NIGHT LIFE
A VAMPS NOVEL

OCT 09

CH

*"THESE BLOODSUCKERS HAVE STYLE."

*Here's what teens and YA bloggers
say about* Vamps:

*"*Vamps* blends the glamour and scandal of high society with the gothic darkness of vampire legend. It's a deliciously vamp-tastic beginning to a series that is well worth keeping up with. I can't wait to sink my teeth into [*Night Life*]. And that's a compliment, coming from a vegetarian."
—sorahikaru13

"Reads like a cross between *Twilight* and *Gossip Girl*."
—kpl_teen_reads

"*Vamps* is a book that has everything I love. It has heroes, villains, cliques, and women empowerment all at the same time. Cally is definitely my kind of girl, and like any good vampire story it keeps you wanting more."
—Kim

"Nancy A. Collins has created a fascinating world that sucks you in and won't let go. With all the mysterious and supernatural happenings at every turn, readers will constantly be wondering what exactly is going on behind the gates of Bathory Academy."—Catherine

NANCY A. COLLINS

HARPER TEEN

AN IMPRINT OF HARPERCOLLINS*PUBLISHERS*

HarperTeen is an imprint of HarperCollins Publishers.

Vamps: Night Life
Copyright © 2009 by Nancy A. Collins
www.harperteen.com

Library of Congress Cataloging-in-Publication Data
Collins, Nancy A.
    Night life / by Nancy A. Collins. — 1st ed.
        p.   cm. — (Vamps)
    Summary: Vampire heiress Lilith Todd flaunts the laws of
her people by starting a career as a fashion model while her half
sister and archrival Cally Monture pursues a forbidden romance
with a vampire hunter.
    ISBN 978-0-06-134918-8 (pbk.)
    [1. Vampires—Fiction. 2. Sisters—Fiction. 3. Social
classes—Fiction. 4. Wealth—Fiction. 5. New York (N.Y.)—
Fiction.] I. Title.
PZ7.C683528Ni 2009   2008014680
[Fic]—dc22   CIP
                                                    AC

Typography by Andrea Vandergrift

❖
First Edition

09 10 11 12 13 CG/RRDH 10 9 8 7 6 5 4 3 2

Dedicated to the memory of my aunt Emily
1930–2006

The Devil hath power
To assume a pleasing shape.
—Shakespeare, *Hamlet*, Act 2, Scene 2

CHAPTER ONE

With its airy, open spaces, Bergdorf Goodman evoked a sense of uncluttered gentility that was a world away from the funky boutiques and consignment stores Cally Monture normally shopped. Indeed, it felt more like a museum, except that she was surrounded by mannequins in slinky evening clothes.

Cally browsed the racks with her new friends from school in search of gowns suitable for the upcoming Rauhnacht Grand Ball—all the while taking mental notes on the textures, lines, forms, and colors used by the high-end labels. With a little luck, she hoped to be able to replicate some of them on her sewing machine at home.

"*Ooh!* What about *this* one?" Cally asked, holding up a sleeveless Dolce & Gabbana black matte jersey gown with a gathered bust and plunging V-line.

"It's very nice, but don't you think it's a little too revealing?" Bella Maledetto frowned.

"Duh!" Melinda Mauvais said. A tall, attractive sixteen-year-old with smooth, mocha-colored skin and smoldering jade-green eyes, she was easily the most exotic of the quartet. "The whole point of the Grand Ball is advertising you're eligible!"

"It's just not my style," Bella insisted.

Cally rolled her eyes, unsurprised by her friend's reply. Bella's fashion sense was nonexistent, and her twin sister Bette's wasn't any better, given that they dressed exactly alike. Not that the whole Tokyopop look didn't work every now and then, but only if you were trying to be *ironic*. The only way anyone could tell them apart was by the color of the ribbons in their hair: blue for Bella, red for Bette. Luckily, the twins were aware they needed all the help they could get, which was why Cally and Melinda had been asked to accompany them.

Cally decided to try her luck with the other sister. "What do you think, Bette?"

"I think it's sexy," Bette said. Since she was ten minutes older than her twin, Bette liked to consider herself more mature.

"You need to pick something out, Bella. After all, the Grand Ball is next weekend!" Melinda reminded her.

"What about you? Do you have something selected for the Grand Ball, Melly?" Cally asked.

"As a matter of fact, my personal shopper called to tell me the alterations to my Valentino are finished. You want to go with me?"

"What about us?" Bella and Bette asked in unison.

"Why don't you go take another look at those Vera Wangs over there?" Cally suggested as Melinda dragged her off in the direction of the alterations department. "We'll catch up with you once we're finished."

"Here you are, Miss Mauvais," the saleslady said.

Melinda unzipped the garment bag and gave the dress a cursory check. She glanced at Cally, who was leaning over her shoulder for a better look. "What do you think?"

"I think it's *gorgeous*, Melly!" Cally said, running her hand over the fabric. As she did, she noticed that the sales tag was still attached. While Melinda turned to speak to the saleswoman, Cally flipped the tag over and stared at the numbers in front of and behind the comma. The ball gown cost the equivalent of three mortgage payments on the condo she and her mother shared in Williamsburg.

"Would you like to try it on in our dressing room to make sure the alterations are correct?" the saleslady asked.

"That won't be necessary," Melinda replied as she reached into her genuine crocodile Hermès bag and handed the saleslady one of her father's business cards.

"I have a seamstress on my staff who can see to it, if necessary. Have it sent to this address."

"Right away, Miss Mauvais."

As they headed back to rejoin the Maledetto sisters, Melinda asked the question Cally had been dreading all afternoon: "So, what are you wearing for Rauhnacht?"

Cally paused, trying to decide whether to tell her friend she had not been invited to attend the Grand Ball as one of the year's debutantes. But it felt so good to be accepted as an equal, and she didn't want to do anything that would ruin the moment or embarrass Melinda by pointing out the social chasm between them.

"I've commissioned an original," she replied offhandedly, hoping it would deflect further inquiry.

"Cool! Anyone I know?"

"I don't think so," Cally lied. "She's just getting started, but she's very promising."

"Rauhnacht is all very sexist and medieval, if you ask me," Melinda said with a sigh. "But I can't bash it *too* hard. After all, it's how my parents met. My grandfather Asema came to the Grand Ball here in New York all the way from Suriname to find a husband for my mother."

"Your mom's from South America? Cool! I didn't know that."

"Since my ancestors came to the New World from West Africa instead of Europe, my totem is a panther, not a wolf. Lilith used to tease me for being different."

"She made catty comments, I take it?" Cally said dryly.

Cally and Melinda succeeded in tracking down the twins, who were dutifully sorting through the various gowns in the Vera Wang section.

"Have you found something you like yet?" Cally asked.

"*I* have," Bette said proudly, holding out a sleeveless black gown with a straight skirt.

"I think you have a winner there, Bette!" Cally said approvingly as she eyed the deep V-neck and ruched waistline. "How about you, Bella? What do you think?"

The other twin shook her head. "I don't like showing off so much skin."

"You know, you don't *have* to wear the same evening gown as Bette," Cally reminded her. "In fact, it's considered a big fashion no-no if you do."

"But we always dress alike," Bella protested. "We're *twins*."

"But that doesn't mean you're the same person. I mean, you two don't have the exact same likes and dislikes, am I right?"

Bella nodded. "She thinks Johnny Depp is cute. I like Orlando Bloom."

"See? That's exactly what I'm talking about!" Cally smiled. "You two might look the same on the outside, but on the inside you're different! And it's time you started letting others know that.

"Bella, how about you go pick out a gown that *you* like by the same designer as Bette? That way you can be the same but still be different."

Bella's face suddenly lit up. "I know *just* the one! Wait here—I'll go get it!"

Melinda shook her head in amazement as she watched Bella scamper off. "I've been trying to talk fashion sense into that girl for weeks, and you manage to get through to her in less than a day!"

"This is the one I liked, but *Bette* said it was boring," Bella said, returning with a sleeveless black satin gown with a gathered neckline, a tiny waist, and a full skirt.

"Very nice," Cally said.

"You *really* like it?" Bella asked anxiously. "You don't think it's dull?"

"I think it's very elegant," Cally assured her.

"*Ooh!* You know what would go *perfect* with that?" Melinda exclaimed, her eyes agleam. "These high-heel Azzaro strappy sandals I saw on sale downstairs!" The smile on Melinda's face suddenly disappeared. "Uh-oh. Bitch alert."

"Where?" the twins said in unison, their heads swiveling like radar dishes.

"Over there." Melinda nodded toward the escalators.

Cally felt her stomach knot as she turned to see Lilith Todd, the most popular and feared student at Bathory

Academy. Nothing turns a fun afternoon of shopping with the girls into a bummer faster than bumping into someone who has recently tried to kill you.

Unlike the school they attended, Bergdorf's wasn't an official vendetta-free zone. However, acting on vendettas in public, especially when plenty of humans were around, was frowned upon by the Synod. That in and of itself was usually enough to guarantee safe passage. Still, when dealing with someone as vindictive and temperamental as Lilith Todd, anything was possible.

"What do we do?" Bette and Bella whispered in tandem, the same worried look on their identical faces. Given that their father was the sworn enemy of Lilith's father, they were also concerned by her unexpected appearance.

"There's no reason to get upset," Cally assured them, trying to keep her voice as calm as possible. "We outnumber her, right?"

"Girls like Lilith *never* shop alone," Melinda said, her eyes darting warily about the store. "They're like cobras—if you see one, assume there are others nearby. See what I mean?"

Cally saw Carmen Duivel, in all her red-haired glory, headed in their direction followed by two other girls. The first girl was stork tall and built like a stick insect, with long, strawberry-blond hair drawn back into a partial upsweep. The second was short and curvy with sleek black hair worn in a Dutch bob that framed her oval face and accented her Cupid's bow mouth.

"Who are they?" Cally asked.

"Armida Aitken is the tall one, and Lula Lumley is the short one," Melinda whispered. "They're from established Old Blood families, although nowhere near as powerful as Lilith's. But then, that's how Lilith likes it. It's good to be the queen bee."

"I think we'd better leave," Bella said anxiously.

"We have *every bit* as much right to be here as she does," Cally replied firmly. "We're still in America, even if we are at Bergdorf's. I'm not going to run away simply because Lilith and her posse are in the same building. . . ."

"Well, well, well!" Lilith's voice was loud enough that nearby customers looked up from their shopping. "It's Three-M: Monture, Mauvais, and Maledetto!"

"Shouldn't that be Four-M?" Armida Aitken asked, counting on her fingers. "There's two Maledettos. . . ."

"*No*, because they're interchangeable as far as I'm concerned!" Lilith hissed over her shoulder, irritated at having to explain her joke to someone who was supposed to laugh at it regardless of whether she got it or not.

As Lilith approached, Melinda and the twins stood firm behind Cally, flanking her on either side. Even if they wanted to back down, there was no way of doing so without appearing weak-blooded.

"I didn't know they allowed mongrels in Bergdorf's." Lilith sniffed, looking at Cally as if she were something she'd just scraped off her Fendis.

"They must, because there's a pack of bitches right in front of me," Cally replied.

"Watch your tongue, Monture," Carmen growled. She stepped forward, glaring menacingly, only to freeze as Melinda moved to stand shoulder to shoulder with Cally.

"This isn't school," Lilith snarled. "There aren't any teachers here to intervene on your behalf, New Blood."

"That's funny, I was about to tell *you* the same thing," Cally shot back.

Lilith's eyes narrowed into slivers of blue ice. "You don't belong here, just like you don't belong at Bathory. We're not interested in sharing our territory with a pack of losers, are we, girls?"

"Bergdorf's is *ours*!" Carmen said with a contemptuous toss of her head. "Beat it while you still can."

"Save the Queen of the Damned act for the spods you bully at school," Cally said. "You don't scare us. What are you and your little clique of Vampire American Princesses going to do? Fly around the fragrance counter? Piss on the rugs in the shoe department to mark your turf? Besides, I don't scare easy."

Cally turned and pointed a finger at a mannequin

dressed in a cashmere sweater. A spark of bluish-white electricity arced from the tip of her index finger, leaving a scorch mark the size of a dime on the nineteen-hundred-dollar garment.

Armida and Lula gasped and exchanged nervous looks, while Carmen flinched and took an involuntary step back.

"Now, if you don't mind," Cally said, pushing past Lilith and her entourage, "as much as I would *love* to continue our little conversation, my friends and I are going to check out some shoes."

Cally was on the escalator before she stopped holding her breath. "Praise the Founders that's over with," she gasped.

"You were *incredible*!" Bella and Bette chimed in unison.

"I've never seen *anyone* stand up to Lilith like that!" Melinda laughed. "And *she* hasn't, either!"

"Do you think the reason she hates me is because she blames me for that friend of hers getting killed—what was her name again?"

"Tanith Graves," Melinda replied. "No, I don't think that's it. Lilith and Tanith were tight, but they weren't *that* tight. If you ask me, I think she's scared of you."

"Scared? Of *me*?"

"You can summon lightning just like that!" Melinda said, snapping her fingers. "No one else our age can do anything close! Of *course* she's scared of you!"

Cally glanced back over her shoulder, a worried look on her face. "I dunno, Melly. I think there's more to it than that, but I can't figure out what. . . ."

"The *nerve* of some people!" Carmen hissed. "Melinda *knew* we'd be here today for the trunk show! It's all her doing, I just know it is! She orchestrated this whole thing!"

"I agree," Lilith groaned. "Imagine! Common, low-life trash like Monture and the Maledettos in Bergdorf's. Is *nothing* sacred?"

If Lilith Todd wrote down a list of all the things she hated, it would be a very long list. It would include, in no particular order: school, not getting her way, sharing, her mother, ugly people, poor people, and spods. But there was no doubt as to what would be at the very top: Cally Monture.

As she watched her archenemy and demi-sister ride the escalator to the shoe department in the company of her clique of pathetic losers, Lilith wasn't surprised that her father had kept his illegitimate daughter unaware of his true identity all this time. Looking back at her own childhood, Lilith realized he had treated her pretty much the same. They had both been brought up like mushrooms: kept in the dark and raised on a diet of bullshit. Now that she had a chance to think about it, Lilith had a new thing to add to the top of her hate list: dear ol' Dad.

Lilith had hoped spending the afternoon shopping for a gown for the Grand Ball would take her mind off her problems, but instead it was rubbing her nose in them. Although her knowledge of who and what Cally really was had shaken her to her very core, Lilith didn't dare reveal the truth to anyone, not even Jules.

Nor could she let anyone know just how deeply she had been affected by the revelation. The moment any of her so-called friends sensed weakness on her part, they would turn on her like jackals taking down a wounded lion. And that included her new "BFF," Carmen Duivel.

Carmen had been bucking to take over as her confidante and first lieutenant even before Tanith's death, and now it seemed Lilith couldn't turn around without being badgered by the redhead. *What are you doing? Where are you going? Is Jules going with you?*

Carmen was proving as irritating as a burlap thong, and almost as far up her butt. Still, it was important that Lilith maintain an entourage, and with Tanith's death and Melinda's defection to the Dork Side, Carmen was the sole remaining member of her original posse. And two people are *not* a posse, which was why she was "test driving" Armida Aitken and Lula Lumley. So far, it was rough going.

"We'll be late if we don't hurry," Carmen said. "I heard Gala will only be there for the first hour or so of the trunk show. I don't want to miss her!"

There were already at least two dozen w
ing about in the section of the store set
trunk show. The group of socialites, trop..,
celebutantes chatted among themselves as they sip..
complimentary cocktails and idly examined the racks
of clothes rolled out for their inspection.

Lilith glanced over at the catered refreshment table,
laden with fresh fruit and cheese trays, trying to hide
her revulsion. The sight of what clots called "food" was
enough to make her stomach turn. She wondered how
they could bring themselves to eat such slop.

The store's fashion director held up her hands for
silence. "Ladies, we here at Bergdorf Goodman are
pleased to introduce a new designer to our collection
this coming spring. Here to speak to you about their
upcoming ready-to-wear line is Maison d'Ombres'
North American executive representative."

Carmen nudged Lilith as a tall, well-built man in
his mid-twenties stepped forward. "He makes Ollie
look like a waiter at Applebee's."

"He's cute"—Lilith shrugged—"but Jules is hotter."

"Jules *is* smoking hot," Carmen agreed.

"What do you mean by that?" Lilith said suspiciously.

"Nothing, Lili," Carmen replied quickly. "I was just
saying, you know."

Seemingly oblivious to the discussion of his relative
hotness, the young exec smiled at the women assembled

before him. "Ladies, allow me to introduce to you the bright young face of Maison d'Ombres—the incomparable Gala!"

From behind one of the racks stepped a stunningly beautiful girl with high, rounded cheekbones, pouty bee-stung lips, sparkling aquamarine eyes, and long hair that spilled down about her shoulders like warm butterscotch. With her long, shapely legs and surfer-girl tan, she looked fresh off the beach at Malibu.

As the model sashayed out into the audience dressed in a ruff-collar blouse paired with a bow-belted dark skirt and a houndstooth trench with rolled sleeves, a photographer with broad shoulders and a neatly trimmed Van Dyck beard swung a 35-mm Nikon digital camera into action. The preferred customers "oohed" and "aahed" appreciatively.

On seeing the camera, Lilith and her entourage shifted about uneasily. Although they still had a few years before they would totally lose the ability to reflect and be photographed, they had been raised to be cautious in the presence of photographic equipment.

The photographer circled Gala like a satellite, his back to the other women in the room. As she watched the photographer click away, Lilith recognized him as the man who had approached her at D&G a couple of weeks earlier.

"Who's the paparazzo?" Lula asked.

"That's no pap, that's Kristof," Carmen explained.

"You know him?" Lilith asked, trying not to let her interest show.

"Not personally. He's this hotshot photographer who's done spreads with Iman, Kate Moss, and Kurkova. He's been signed to work on the Maison d'Ombres launch. Speaking of which—what do you think of the clothes?"

Lilith glanced over at the racks full of sample clothing. The garments all seemed to be very well made, but they weren't anything special. "I could vomit something more interesting," she said with a shrug. "Did I mention that I'm to be the last debutante presented at the Grand Ball?"

"Several times," Armida replied.

"I'm looking for something that will rivet every eye in that ballroom. After all, being the final presentation of the evening is very important. The Grand Ball can't begin before I start the first dance of the night. I want a gown that signifies that importance."

As she spoke, Lilith watched some girls come up to the model with paper and pen in hand, seeking autographs. The model scribbled her name, and her admirers eagerly bore the signatures away as if they were as precious as gold.

"I hear Gala signed a million-dollar contract with Maison d'Ombres to be their official model for the next year," Lula whispered. "Spreads in *ELLE*, *Vanity Fair*, and *Vogue* . . . that kind of thing."

"A million?" Lilith tapped her chin with a pearl-pink nail. "How old would you say she is?"

"Seventeen, I guess; maybe eighteen."

"Would you say she's prettier than me?"

"Uhhh . . ." Lula glanced about, not sure how to respond.

"Definitely not!" Carmen protested, quickly stepping into the void created by Lula's gaffe. "You're *much* prettier than her! Most models would *kill* for your looks!"

As Kristof continued to snap pictures, Lilith thought about how her wealth and popularity were not of her own making, but of her father's. She was like the moon, which has no light of its own but merely reflects the light of the sun. Up until now, she had been content to remain within her father's orbit, echoing his glory. But now that she knew she was not his only child, things no longer seemed as certain as they had before.

Perhaps it was time she started shining on her own.

CHAPTER TWO

Rest Haven was one of the few remaining private graveyards in Williamsburg. Behind its ancient brick wall sat an acre of quiet greenery and sun-bleached marble monuments. At night the wrought iron gate was secured against those who would profane the eternal slumber of its permanent residents. Of course, that is not to say the dead who made Rest Haven their final home did not receive callers now and then. Indeed, over the last few weeks the old cemetery had been paid frequent visits by a certain pair of young lovers seeking shelter from the outside world.

As Cally wound her way through the tombstones, she took a deep breath, savoring the smell of the autumn leaves. A fingernail moon hung in the clear October sky, signaling the end of what had been, despite the brief run-in with Lilith Todd, an excellent day. She glanced down at the single lavender Bergdorf's bag she was carrying. Inside it was a matching La Perla Red Carpet bra-and-thong set that cost her almost $350. When she'd paid for the lingerie, she had done so with cash, handing over a fistful of twenties and tens to the saleslady. From the looks on Melinda's and the twins' faces it was clear they had never paid for anything without using plastic.

Still, despite the vast differences in their lifestyles, Cally really liked Melinda and the twins. And they seemed to genuinely like her as well. So it kind of bothered her that she'd spent the whole day lying to them.

Nobody likes getting lied to, but sometimes there's no way around it, especially if you want to stay alive. Lying about being invited to the Grand Ball didn't fall into the survival category. But the biggest lie of them all was actually more a *secret*: her boyfriend was a vampire hunter. And not just *any* vampire hunter, an actual *Van Helsing*. Peter, to be exact.

Yeah, being attracted to a man whose family was sworn to eradicate her race from the earth was beyond cliché, not to mention *seriously* unhealthy. But the moment she had seen Peter in the subway, she'd realized there was something between them. She wasn't sure *what* it was, but the bond was as undeniable as it was forbidden. And it wasn't just one way, either: Peter felt the same immediate attraction, going so far as to track her down after that first meeting in order to tell her how he felt. It was like there were magnets in their hearts that kept drawing them together, no matter how hard they fought against the pull. Whatever it was that drew them together—chemistry, destiny, lust, or fate—all Cally knew was that she couldn't resist.

Being half vampire and half human, she had spent her entire life torn between two worlds, never truly belonging to either one. All those public service announcements telling kids to "just be yourself" made it sound so damned easy. But what if being "yourself" gets you beat up, or even killed, what *then*? Finally, with Peter, she had found someone with whom she didn't have to pretend she was something she wasn't. Sneaking off to be with Peter was like taking a vacation from her real life. When she was with him, she was free to talk about all kinds of things she never could before, like her curiosity about the true identity of her father and the mixture of aggravation and love she felt for her mother. When they were together, all the things that stressed her out seemed to melt away.

At first their rendezvous were infrequent. Now they could barely go a day without seeing each other—despite the danger to both of them should they be discovered.

As Cally approached the hawthorn tree that stood silent sentinel over her grandparents' graves, she spotted a red-and-black-plaid wool blanket spread out on the ground underneath its gnarled branches. Sitting in the middle of the blanket was an old-fashioned wicker picnic hamper. She stopped and looked around. Peter suddenly stepped out from behind one of the nearby monuments. He was older than Cally by a couple of years, with tousled reddish-brown hair and dark brown eyes.

"I thought it would be nice to have a picnic together while the weather's still good," he said with a sheepish smile.

"You really didn't have to do something like this— but I'm glad you did!" Cally said, throwing her arms around his neck.

"I guess I'm just a romantic at heart," he said as they sat down together on the blanket.

"So what kind of picnic did you pack?" Cally grinned, flipping open the lid of the hamper.

"Oh, a little bit of this, a little bit of that," Peter replied. "Let's see . . . we've got a mini-bottle of sparkling Blanc de Blanc, farmhouse biscuits, chocolate truffles . . ."

"What's this?" Cally asked, holding up a stainless steel cylinder. "Coffee?"

"No." Peter chuckled. "That's for you. Go ahead and open it."

Cally unscrewed the top of the gleaming thermos. Even before she looked inside, the smell told her of its contents. She looked up at Peter, who was watching her expectantly.

"Do you like it?" he asked.

"Peter—where did you *get* this?" she asked in an awed whisper.

"It came from the infirmary at the Institute."

Cally screwed the cap back onto the thermos. "Are you *sure* about this, Peter?"

"They'll never notice it's gone," he replied. "I hacked into Doc Willoughby's computer and 'corrected' his inventory. He'll never miss a spare pint of O positive."

Peter reached up and cupped the back of her head in the palm of his hand, running his fingers through her short, dark hair. After a long moment, they finally broke their kiss and stared into each other's eyes.

"You're so beautiful, Cally. I wish I could show you off to the rest of the world." Peter sighed as he stroked her cheek. "I know this little Italian place, with a strolling accordionist and opera singer, just like in *Lady and the Tramp*. It's kinda cheesy, but it's also wicked romantic, you know?"

"It sounds *wonderful*, Peter!" Cally smiled as she busied herself with opening the bottle of wine. "But I couldn't really eat anything, no matter where we end up going. I mean, I could pretend to, like they've been teaching us at school. All I have to do is push my food around on my plate and sneak some of it into my napkin when nobody's looking every now and then, just like anorexics and fashion models do.

"You know, it's been *years* since I went on a picnic. It was up at Granny's cabin in the Catskills. I could still eat solid food back then," she said as she handed him a glass filled with the sparkling wine.

"Are you sure you can't have any of this?" Peter asked, holding out one of the chocolate truffles.

Cally shook her head and pushed the proffered candy away. "If I try, I get sick. I'm on a liquid diet for the rest of my life." She held up a glass identical to the one she'd given him, except this one was filled with chilled blood. "I propose a toast: to us!"

"To us!" Peter agreed. He touched the rim of his wineglass to hers, only to look away at the last moment as Cally drank. "So—how was your day?"

"It was great—but you don't really want to hear about it because it was mostly shopping."

"You're right about that part." Peter chuckled. "You didn't run into any handsome young vampires while you were at it?"

"Are you kidding? Vampire guys aren't *that* different from the rest of you! But I did have a run-in with Lilith Todd."

Peter froze. "Victor Todd's daughter?"

"You know who Victor Todd is?" Cally asked, surprised.

"I know the names of all the major Old Blood families in this city," he replied. "*Especially* the Todds."

"Really? Did I tell you Lilith totally tried to kill me at school?"

"I'm not surprised," Peter said darkly. "The Todds have a mean streak. I should know. Victor murdered my grandfather Leland."

"Oh, Peter! I'm so sorry!" Cally gasped, placing a hand on his arm.

"Todd killed him right in front of my dad. He was about my age when it happened. If it hadn't been for your grandmother Sina, my dad probably would have been killed, too. So, in a way, she's responsible for me being alive."

"That's so weird." Cally shook her head in disbelief. "I'm still trying to get my brain around Granny being a vampire hunter, back in the day."

"*That's* weirder than her being a witch?"

"Hey, I *knew* she was a witch. That was never a secret from me. Besides, I'm a half vampire, so being a witch isn't *that* weird."

"Point taken."

There was a long silence, and then Cally glanced back up at Peter, an anxious look on her face. "Is your dad still trying to find me?"

"Don't worry; he doesn't know where you live or anything like that."

"Yeah, but *you* managed to track me down, didn't you?"

"I changed the files after I hacked into the database. According to the New York State graves registry, your grandparents are now interred at Woodlawn Cemetery, up in the Bronx. You have nothing to worry about, Cally, I *promise*." Peter smiled, giving her hand a comforting squeeze.

"Have you discovered why he's so obsessed with capturing me?"

Peter shook his head. "Just because I'm his son, that doesn't mean he tells me anything about his plans."

"I know how *that* goes." Cally sighed, rolling her eyes. She snuggled in close to him, savoring the warmth of his body pressed against hers. "Peter—do you think there's a place for us in this world?"

"Yes," he said as he gently stroked her hair. "There has to be. Why would we have found each other like we did if there was no hope for happiness for us? Life can't be *that* cruel. Maybe we could run away together to someplace where no one knows who we are. Or better yet, some remote island paradise where the people have never even *heard* of vampires or vampire hunters. We could make love on the beach every night. How does that sound?"

"Like a dream." As she rested her head on his shoulder, Cally pictured herself and Peter walking hand in hand along a shore as white as sugar, watching the moonlight reflect across the ocean. She kissed his neck, savoring his musky smell and the salty taste of his skin on her lips. She felt a rising heat in her belly, born of lust instead of hunger. Even though they had grown increasingly intimate over the last couple of weeks, Cally had yet to taste Peter's blood for fear of losing control and accidentally draining him. Besides, she didn't want to be the first to broach the subject. If he offered up his throat for a love bite, she would have to rethink things. However, she did not want to put pressure on him. After all, it was *his* blood. Still, there were moments when he was sitting so close, she could feel the blood rushing through his arteries and veins. If she listened really hard, she could almost hear it calling out to her, tempting her to take just one sip. . . . *What could it hurt? Besides, you know he wants it, too.* . . . Cally shuddered, forcing her thoughts from the path they were on.

"Is something wrong?" Peter asked, unaware of what had been running through her mind.

"No," she lied. "I was just thinking about what you said about your grandfather. I never knew there was so much bad blood between the Van Helsings and the Todds. It sounds like the vendettas that go on between vampire families. You must *really* hate the Todds."

"Just the ones who deserve it," he replied.

As Cally entered the lobby of her apartment building, she spotted Mr. Dithers, the chairman of the condo association, emptying his trash into the incinerator chute. She walked as fast as she could toward the elevator, praying it was sitting on the lobby level for once instead of hanging around on the seventh floor. She punched the call button and, to her relief, the doors parted instantly.

"Miss Monture—! A moment, please?"

Cally turned to find Mr. Dithers standing at her elbow, his Coke-bottle glasses making his over-magnified eyes appear to be hovering in front of his face.

"We've been getting complaints from the tenants on either side of your unit—and those on the floors above and below as well, to be frank—about the noise from your home entertainment center. I've already sent two warning notices to your mother. . . ."

"I realize that, Mr. Dithers," Cally said apologetically. "I'm *really* sorry. I'll talk to my mother about keeping it down—"

"It's not that I have anything against you personally, Cally. I *know* you try the best you can, but the noise ordinances are built into the covenants of the condo board. If this continues, we'll have no choice but to fine your mother two hundred dollars for each new complaint."

"There's no need to get drastic," Cally assured him. "I'll take care of the situation, I promise."

"I certainly hope so, Miss Monture."

As the elevator doors opened onto her floor, Cally was relieved she could not hear whatever movie her mother was watching from halfway down the hall. She unlocked the door and stepped inside the apartment. The combination kitchen-dining area was dark, save for the faint bluish-white light from the living room.

"Mom—? I just ran into Mr. Dithers again," Cally announced as she set her purse on the breakfast bar.

Cally's mother was seated on a red velvet chaise lounge, watching the hi-def plasma flat screen hung on the living room wall. As she entered the room, Cally realized why everything was so uncharacteristically quiet: her mother was watching F. W. Murnau's classic silent film *Nosferatu*.

"Mom? Did you hear me? We need to talk."

"Damn *right* we need to talk!" Sheila Monture said as she turned to glare at her daughter. "I want to know where you've been sneaking off to at all hours, young lady! You're seeing someone, aren't you?"

"Mom, you've been drinking," Cally said in a matter-of-fact voice. "You *know* I won't talk about things like this when you're drunk."

Sheila pushed herself up off the chaise lounge, teetering for a moment until she regained her balance. She was dressed in a long, flowing black velvet dress with tight-fitting long sleeves that ended in a point above the hand, with lace finger loops affixed to the cuffs. Cally recognized the outfit, and the long black wig that went with it, as the Morticia Addams look her mother favored whenever she obsessed about their social standing in the vampire community. This was a real laugh, seeing how her mom was a human.

"Just because I'm asleep by the time you normally come traipsing home doesn't mean I don't notice things! You better not be messing around with that no-account Johnny Muerto! I won't have you ruining your chances of finding a proper husband by fooling with that newbie trash!"

Cally rolled her eyes in disgust. "Mom, I *despise* Johnny Muerto! I got sent to Professor Burke's office for punching him in the throat when he tried to kiss me, remember?"

"Well, if you're not sneaking off with him, then which one of those Varney Hall newbies *are* you fooling around with?" Sheila asked.

"I'm not seeing *any* New Blood boy on the sly, Mom! Besides, I don't know what you're so worried about. Oldies only marry their own kind, and I'm definitely not one of *them*!"

"You shouldn't talk like that about yourself, sweetie," Sheila admonished, leaning forward to stroke her daughter's hair. "You're as good as *any* of those Old Blood girls you go to school with. Those boys at Ruthven's would be falling all over themselves if they knew who your father was!"

"Yeah, big help *that* is," Cally said acidly, pushing her mother's hand away from her face. When Sheila was this close, it was impossible to ignore the reek of bourbon. "*I* don't even know who my father really is!"

"He's a very rich and powerful member of Old Blood society. . . ." Sheila said, as if reciting from memory.

"Yeah, that's what you *always* say, Mom, but you *still* won't tell me his name!" Cally replied angrily. "I'm going to be seventeen pretty soon, and I still don't know who my dad is! Don't you think it's time you finally told me? Why are you still protecting him?"

"You know I can't tell you that, Cally," Sheila said, her shoulders slumping wearily. "Your grandmother made me . . ." She looked away without finishing her sentence. "It's for your own good, sugar."

"You *always* try to put it off on Granny when I ask you about my father's identity!" Cally snapped. "I'm tired of you blaming her! Granny's been dead for two years now. You could tell me his name if you wanted to; the truth is, you *won't*!"

"Cally, sweetie, you don't understand how it is with your father—"

"No, I *don't*! And it looks like I never will if I have to rely on you for information! I'm going to my room now—oh, and Mom, don't call New Bloods 'newbies,' okay? It's rude. How would you like it if I called you a *clot*?" Cally slammed the door to her room so hard it shook the entire floor.

So much for the noise ordinance.

CHAPTER THREE

Lilith Todd walked up the imposing granite stairs that led to the doors of the Belfry. She paused to glance at the throngs of bridge-and-tunnel wannabes gathered on the wrong side of the velvet ropes, hoping against hope that they would be permitted access to the former fin de siècle church, now the hottest club in town. Outfitted in a blush Dolce & Gabbana corset dress and open-toe Manolo pumps, she was the beautiful people personified.

As far as Lilith was concerned, all clots were clueless, but some were definitely worse than others. Like, really, who would wear a cheap red top and a cheaper black skirt bought ten years ago at Sears out to a night-club? Not that it mattered, because that tacky little creature certainly wasn't getting inside tonight, or any other night. Her boyfriend wasn't any better, what with the long, purple leather coat he was wearing. Did that dude think he was going to a rave? How lame! She put her hand over her mouth, just in case she accidentally popped her fangs while laughing at them.

Breezing past the hulking doorman, she made her way through those who had gathered to see and be seen as they danced, drank, and drugged the night away. She really needed a pick-me-up, and although there were at least three bars on the main floor of the club, none of them served her favorite drink.

As she climbed the stairs to the converted choir loft that served as the club's VIP room, the ear-hammering dance music dropped down to a muted roar. She spotted her boyfriend, Jules de Laval, lounging on one of the divans scattered about the room, talking to two of his friends and fellow students at Ruthven's, Sergei Savanovic and Oliver Drake. With his artfully mussed mane of reddish-gold hair, strong jaw, and lambent green eyes, he resembled a virile young king holding court.

"How was your afternoon with Armida and Lula?" Jules asked.

"One's a short little dwarf and the other looks like a tranny," Lilith replied, kissing the air beside Jules's cheek so she wouldn't ruin her makeup. "Going shopping with them was like watching blood dry, only not as fun."

"I take it they failed the audition?"

"I didn't say that," Lilith said quickly. "I'll tell you more after I get a drink."

"You're going to be Lilith's escort at the Grand Ball, right?" Sergei asked as he watched Lilith walk over to the VIP bar. His eyes were riveted on her hips, beautifully outlined by the blush corset dress she was wearing. Although he had the deep, dark eyes of a poet, Sergei dressed like a rock star and had the sexual appetite to match.

"Nope."

"Why not?"

"It's against the rules. Debutantes can't be escorted by someone they're romantically involved with. It's some stupid tradition. And since Lili and I are promised, that counts me out. Ask Ollie: he can't escort Carmen, either."

"Jules is right," Oliver said. With his dirty-blond hair and boyish face he seemed as harmless as a puppy dog, until you looked into his flinty eyes. "So who *are* you escorting to the Grand Ball, Jules?"

"It's up to the girls to ask the guys to be their escort, not the other way around," Jules said. "You know that."

"I don't get it," Oliver said suspiciously. "You're telling us that not *one* of the girls has asked *you*—the most lusted-after boy at Ruthven's—to be her escort to the Grand Ball?"

"You know Lilith—she doesn't share," Jules said with

a shrug. "None of the other girls are willing to risk her getting jealous by asking me. How about you, Sergei? Have any of the girls asked you to be their escort?"

"Sort of," Sergei said, shooting a glance in Oliver's direction. "It sort of depends on what someone else says."

By the time Lilith reached the bar, the bartender already had her drink poured and waiting for her: AB neg, laced with bourbon, served at body temperature with a hint of anticoagulant; just the way she liked it.

As she took her first sip, the man standing next to her at the bar smiled and winked at her in what he thought was a debonair opening move. He was in his late thirties, his slightly overfed face flushed from drinking, and he smelled strongly of cologne. Compared to the sleekly fashionable club goers he was attempting to mingle with, he looked boring and old—a stockbroker out on the town.

"Sure you can handle a drink like that, little lady?" he asked, pointing at what he thought was a glass of wine.

Lilith coughed into her fist, trying not to laugh out loud. "Don't worry," she said, giving the glass a slight hoist. "I've been drinking this stuff since I was a baby."

As Lilith turned to rejoin her friends, the stockbroker, emboldened by the alcohol he'd been downing, reached out and grabbed her elbow.

"I was thinking—after you finish your drink, maybe I could buy you another one?"

Lilith looked down at the wedding ring on the man's finger, then fixed him with a stare as blue and cold as ice pulled from the heart of Antarctica. "I'm here with my fiancé," she said flatly.

The stockbroker saw a blond youth with the body of a surfer sitting on a nearby divan, watching him with eyes that seemed strangely luminescent in the dim light, like those of a jungle beast. The young man had a slight smile on his face that was far from friendly.

"Sorry," the stockbroker said quickly, releasing her arm.

"You should be." Lilith sniffed. "Go back to Connecticut while you still can, family guy."

The stockbroker slunk back to his place at the bar, looking glum as he motioned to the bartender for another drink.

"Did you see that clot?" Lilith said as she rejoined the group. "Seb's really slipping if *that's* what he's allowing into the VIP room nowadays. That guy is *so* gross!"

"I wouldn't worry about it," Sergei replied. He eyed the human seated at the bar. "Your admirer is probably headed for the cellar."

"I hope he's A poz and drinks scotch." Jules sighed wistfully. "The only donor the club has on scotch right now is a B neg. Seb swears up and down that the clot's on an intravenous drip of Glenlivet 21 Year Old, but it might as well be rotgut as far as I'm concerned."

"So what were you talking about while I was getting hit on by Mr. Wife-and-Two-Kids-in-Danbury?" Lilith asked.

"Nothing, really," Oliver said. "We were just discussing the Grand Ball."

"Don't remind me!" She groaned. "I still haven't found a decent gown!"

"You didn't buy anything today?" Jules asked, surprised.

"Of *course* I bought something!" Lilith said, rolling her eyes in disdain. "I found these *really* gorgeous Louboutin knotted platform mules and this really, *really* cute Derek Lam dress in French navy blue with buttons down along the right side, oh, and this really, really, *really* sweet matching blue quilted patent leather Marc Jacobs satchel. I just didn't see a *gown* I liked, that's all."

"Well, as long as it wasn't a wasted trip," Jules said.

"You know, I was thinking it might be nice to go back to your place tonight," Lilith said with a wink. "Your parents are still out of town, aren't they? And we had such a nice time the other night. . . ."

"We *can* do that, if that's what you want," Jules replied hesitantly. "But—"

"But what?"

"We won't be alone, that's all. Aunt Juliana and Uncle

Boris are getting their home out in the Hamptons ready for the Grand Ball, so Xander's staying with us for the time being."

"Ugh. Never mind! I couldn't get comfortable with Exo hanging around. Maybe even peeping through the keyhole, for all I know." Lilith shuddered at the thought of Xander Orlock seeing her naked. "Couldn't you tell him to get lost or something?"

"Lili, you're going to have to get used to having Exo around," Jules said wearily. "He's my cousin, after all. Eventually he's going to be part of *your* family, too, at least by marriage."

"Don't remind me." Lilith scowled.

"I've never been out to the Orlocks' estate in the Hamptons," Oliver said. "What's it like?"

"King's Stone is pretty cool. Exo told me that it's supposed to be modeled on a castle or something from the Old Country. Uncle Boris had it built from stone blocks quarried from the Carpathians. The place is *humongous*! When me and Exo were kids, we used to play hide-and-seek there all the time."

"I need another drink," Lilith announced loudly, holding up her empty glass and wagging it at Jules.

"Your legs don't look broken to me," he replied, turning back to his conversation with Oliver.

Lilith's eyes narrowed and her jaw clenched. Typical Jules! One minute he was all over her, lighting candles and giving her back rubs and jewelry, the next he acted like he couldn't be bothered to remember her name. Lilith got up from the divan and stormed off in search of a fresh drink.

As she returned to the bar, the stockbroker who had accosted her earlier slowly raised his head and stared at Lilith. The lust that had burned in his eyes was now extinguished and replaced with anguish. It was the look of a man who realized that he'd passed into dangerous territory and had no clue how to get back to safer ground.

"Something . . . in my drink," he managed to slur as he tried to step away from the stool, only to have his legs buckle underneath him.

Suddenly Sebastian was there at the stockbroker's side, catching him under the arms before the clot could hit the ground. Although the club promoter didn't weigh more than one hundred and twenty pounds and wore outlandishly high platform shoes, he had no trouble hoisting the drunk back onto his seat unassisted.

"Andre, Christian—please escort our friend here to the cellar," Sebastian said to the bodybuilders-cum-bouncers flanking him. "Quentin—what was he drinking?"

"Scotch," the bartender replied.

"Perfect!" Sebastian smiled, flashing a set of pearly white fangs. "Andre, set our new donor up on a Bushmills IV drip."

"Ten or Sixteen?"

"Start him out on the ten-year-old," the promoter replied. "I'll decide whether to step him up or not after he's been typed."

"Gotcha, boss."

Lilith sipped on her new drink as she watched the bodybuilders drag the clot behind the tapestries hanging along the back wall to the hidden door that led directly to the cavernous basement underneath the club. As far as the humans lounging in the Loft were concerned, the staff were merely escorting yet another over-served patron off the premises, but the truth was far stranger—and darker—than anything they could ever imagine.

She wondered if she should hurry back to the others but decided she was still too pissed at Jules. The way he ran hot and cold with her was enough to make her tear her hair. Didn't he know how lucky he was to have her? He said he hated it when she got jealous, yet it seemed as if he wasn't happy when she *wasn't*. There was no pleasing him. If her father hadn't signed that marriage contract with Count de Laval, she would be sorely tempted to dump Jules's perfect, sculpted ass for someone more supportive. But who? Lilith had spent her entire life visualizing herself as Jules's spouse and the next Countess de Laval. The thought of being with anyone else was as alien to her as the concept of sharing.

"Lilith, my dear!" Sebastian said, turning his full attention to the beautiful blond heiress. "You must have sneaked in while my back was turned! You *know* you're not supposed to come into the club without giving me a kiss!"

"I would never forget something like that, Seb." Lilith laughed, kissing the air next to his powdered and rouged cheek.

"Now you have to tell me how much you missed me since the *last* time you were here! You *did* miss me, didn't you, darling?"

"Of course I missed you, Seb! I *always* miss you."

"Hang on a moment," he said, putting a finger to the Bluetooth earpiece clipped onto his left ear. "I've got an incoming. Yeah, Tomás—what is it? *Really?* Where is she?"

"What's going on?" Lilith asked, her curiosity piqued.

"We've got a celeb on the way up to the Loft."

"One of ours or one of theirs?"

"One of *theirs*. Some hot little fashion model named Gala."

"*Gala?*" Lilith raised an eyebrow. "I just saw her at the trunk show at Bergdorf's this afternoon."

"You lucky little bitch! I *never* get to go shopping anymore. I have to order most of my ensembles online. I would love to chat more, but I have to make sure the staff knows that our little celebrity is Off The Menu.

Ah! There she is!" Sebastian said, tottering off as fast as his platform shoes could carry him.

Lilith watched as the club promoter approached the model, fawning over her like a dog eager to ingratiate itself with a pack leader. Gala had exchanged the bland Maison d'Ombres threads she'd worn at the show for a metallic silver halter dress with matching strappy high heels that showed off her sun-kissed skin and toned body. Lilith felt a flare of jealousy as she realized that Sebastian was greeting Gala exactly like he'd welcomed her.

As the model moved through the room, every head turned to follow her. When she sat down, her barely there skirt rode up, revealing panties to match. The eyes of the men shone with lust, while those of the women flashed with envy—especially Lilith's.

"What's all the excitement about?"

Lilith was startled by the sound of Jules's voice in her ear. She had been so focused on the attention Gala was getting, she had failed to notice Jules walking up behind her.

"It's nothing, just some model named Gail something, I think."

"Really?" Oliver stood on tiptoe in order to get a better view. "Is she hot?"

"Of *course* she's hot," Sergei replied, rolling his eyes. "She's a model. *Duh!*"

Oliver nudged Sergei in the ribs. "Wanna go check her out?"

"I don't know why you're in such a hurry to go ogle some tarted-up clot." Lilith sniffed.

"Jealous much, Lili?" Sergei snickered.

"What's there to be jealous of? If her tan was any oranger, she'd be an Oompa-Loompa!"

"She *still* looks hot," Sergei said with a shrug.

"Whatever!" Lilith snapped. "Excuse me—I need to put on some lipstick."

The ladies' room in the Loft, unlike its sister downstairs, did not have a vanity mirror over the sink. Normally Lilith would bring Tanith or one of the other girls with her so that they could check each other's makeup, but Tanith was dead, Melinda had defected, and she'd had enough of Carmen for the day, thank you very much. Without a spotter, she did not dare apply any more lipstick. But then, she hadn't really needed to fix her makeup in the first place. She'd simply had enough of the others drooling over that bimbo model.

Just then Gala entered the ladies' room like she was striding down a runway in Milan. She passed Lilith without a single glance and disappeared into one of the stalls.

Lilith turned the sink faucet on with her elbow and began to pretend to wash her hands. A minute later she was rewarded by the sound of a flushing toilet and the stall door reopening. She pulled a length of brown paper towel from the dispenser, taking her time drying hands that had never been wet. She then stepped out of the way, allowing the model access to the sink.

"I saw you at the trunk show," Lilith said, the words tumbling out faster than she'd intended.

"Yeah?" Gala said in a politely bored voice as she stuck her hands under the running water.

"I was wondering—can I ask you a question?"

Gala shrugged but did not bother to look up at Lilith.

"What do you think of Kristof?"

Gala turned off the water and looked sideways at Lilith. There was a hard glint in the model's aquamarine eyes that Lilith had not seen before. "What *about* Kristof?"

"I'm just asking if he's any good? I'm thinking of taking up an offer to pose for him—"

"*You?* Pose for Kristof?" Gala ran her eyes up and down Lilith's body like it was a dirty rag. "There's this magazine called *Vogue*, sweetie—you better pick it up and thumb through it before you go wasting Kristof's time."

As Gala walked out of the ladies' room, she thought she heard the low, throaty growl of an angry dog. But that was ridiculous. What would an animal like that be doing in a Manhattan nightclub?

Gala already had a realtor lining up a new place for her that was more befitting her rising supermodel status, but until something opened up she still split the rent three ways with two other models from her agency, living in an apartment in Chelsea.

As the taxi pulled away from the curb, she was momentarily startled by what she thought was someone standing in the shadows of the doorway of her building. She gasped in fear, but when she looked again, the figure had disappeared.

Damn it, Skyler, you better not have palmed off acid as X on me again, she thought sourly as she unlocked the door to the lobby. She had that shoot with Kristof first thing Monday, and the last thing she needed was to spend the next eighteen hours tripping. Kristof hated it when his models arrived for a shoot looking tired and worn out.

It was one thing to pretend she was partying her ass off for the cameras; it was quite another to look like she'd just closed down the last bar on the Bowery.

As Gala walked past the bank of mailboxes in the lobby, she had the weirdest feeling that she was being watched. She glanced over her shoulder but saw nothing. Still, she couldn't shake the sensation that someone, or some*thing*, had been behind her.

Damn it, Skyler! Dosed again!

She punched the call button and heard the elevator start to make its way back down from one of the upper floors. As she waited for it to arrive, she consoled herself with thoughts of all the nice things she was going to buy herself with the money from the Maison d'Ombres contract.

After what felt like an eternity spent modeling expensive cars, clothes, shoes, perfumes, and jewelry, she was finally going to be able to afford them. Not bad for a high school dropout from Ledbetter, Texas, with nothing but a GED and some kick-ass genes to her credit.

The doors to the elevator opened, revealing pitch-black darkness. At first she thought the bulb inside the car must have burned out, but as she stepped in, Gala heard broken glass crunch under her foot. Someone had shattered the overhead light.

Gala quickly stepped back out of the elevator. The very idea of being sealed inside a pitch-black box, even for a few seconds, was enough to give her the chills, tripping or not. For all she knew, whoever broke the light was still in there, watching her from the darkness.

Cursing under her breath, she began climbing the stairs to her fifth-floor apartment. The building was prewar and the steps were worn from generations of foot traffic up and down their flights. One thing was for certain, in her new building—wherever that might be—this kind of thing would never happen. Supermodels didn't take the stairs.

As she reached the third floor, Gala heard the scuffing of a foot on the landing above her. She paused and leaned out past the banister, looking up the narrow shaft of the stairwell. To her surprise, she saw some-one peering back down at her from the fifth floor. She instantly recoiled, her heart racing in her chest, and began frantically fishing around inside her Gucci tote. She sighed in relief as her fingers closed around her cell phone.

She was about to punch in 911 when it suddenly occurred to her that calling the police might not be the smartest thing to do. After all, she was underage, drunk, and on drugs. While she wasn't sure she'd *really* seen someone looking back at her from the landing above, she was dead certain she couldn't pass a breatha-lyzer test. She was probably just seeing things. She *was* tripping, after all.

Mustering up her courage, Gala edged over and peered up the stairwell. No one was looking back down at her. With a sigh of relief, she returned the cell to her purse and resumed her climb.

As she reached the landing, there was a loud flap-ping sound, like laundry on a clothesline snapping in a high wind, and something large and dark came swoop-ing down the stairs. Before she could react, Gala found herself being pummeled by huge, leathery wings. The thing attacking her thrust its face into hers, revealing a hideous mix of bat and human features: short, piglike nose, beady eyes, and gnashing fangs.

Gala screamed and clapped her hands over her eyes in a desperate attempt to blot out the horror before her.

As she spun around, the heel of her shoe abruptly gave way, sending her tumbling down the steps. She came to rest on the next landing, her legs bent like those of a broken doll.

She moaned in pain as she lifted her head, blood trickling from the corner of her mouth, only to freeze upon seeing that her attacker was crouched over her like a vulture. The model opened her mouth to scream, but she was so frightened all she could manage was a choking noise.

The creature's monstrous features seemed to waver, as if seen through a haze of rising heat, and, to her surprise, Gala suddenly found herself looking into the face of a beautiful young girl with cold blue eyes and long honey-blond hair.

"*Nobody* talks to me like that and gets away with it," the bat-girl snarled. She grinned, revealing a pair of white canines that grew bigger and bigger the longer she smiled. "Kristof is *mine*, bitch."

Before the creature could sink her fangs into Gala's throat, there was the sound of a door being thrown open.

"Who's there?" a man's voice called out.

The bat-girl yanked her head back, hissing in anger. And just as suddenly as she had appeared, she was gone. In her place was an older man Gala recognized as one of her neighbors, dressed in a loosely belted bathrobe and carrying a hockey stick as an impromptu weapon.

"Oh my God! I'll call nine-one-one!"

Gala looked up and saw the bat-girl hanging from the ceiling over the Good Samaritan's head like a monstrous chandelier, grinning down at her with demonic glee.

Only then was she finally able to scream.

CHAPTER FOUR

It was early Sunday evening and Cally was in her room. As she finished sewing the zipper into a black miniskirt, her home phone rang. Setting aside her scissors and thread, she picked it up before it could roll over to voice mail.

"Hey there, girl," Melinda said, not bothering to identify herself.

"Hi, Melly. What's up?"

"Nothing much. I was wondering if you wanted to go check out this new club tonight. I used to party at the Belfry, but I need a new place to hang. Scuttlebutt has it that the Viral Room is a VIP club."

"VIPs?" Cally frowned.

"You know: *Vampires Into Partying.*" Melinda laughed. "What about it? Wanna check it out?"

"Are Bella and Bette coming?"

"Those two? *Clubbing?* Are you serious?"

"Okay, I'm game. I need an excuse to get out of the house—my mom has been driving me nuts!"

"I hear that. When do you think you'll be ready? I can send a car around for you. . . ."

"No, that's okay," Cally replied quickly. The last thing she needed was one of her friends accidentally getting a look at her mother. "I'll meet you there. How's midnight sound?"

"Great. The witching hour it is. See you at the club."

Her mother, as usual, was reclining on the red velvet chaise lounge in front of the television. Tonight she was watching *Near Dark* with a pair of wireless headphones clamped over her ears in grudging concession to the condo board's most recent complaints.

Cally leaned over and lifted one of the headphones, speaking directly into her mother's ear. "Mom, I'm going out to the clubs tonight."

"Don't forget to pick up the laundry from the cleaners first," Sheila replied. "I had them dry-clean your school blazer. Honestly, Cally, it looked like you'd worn it to a slaughterhouse! Next time try and be more careful when you open the blood packets the school gives you for lunch."

"Don't worry, Mom, I will," Cally promised. She was relieved that her mother did not question her explanation for the bloodstains. If she knew that her daughter had been attacked while at school—by Lilith

Todd, no less—Sheila would freak.

"That's nice, sweetie," Sheila replied, unaware that she was talking to an empty room.

Lilith sat on the corner of her bed, staring at the number printed on Kristof's business card. Marshaling her courage, she quickly punched the numbers into her cell phone before her resolve could fade.

The phone on the other end of the line rang. And rang. And rang. She was afraid the call might go to voice mail when she suddenly heard an older, masculine voice.

"Hello?"

"I'm trying to reach Kristof . . . ?"

"Speaking."

Lilith never got nervous around humans. In her mind, nervousness was connected to fear. And with the exception of Van Helsings, what did she have to fear from humans? After all, she was faster, stronger, deadlier, and prettier than all of them, wasn't she? However, for some reason she found her mouth dry as cotton as she spoke.

"This might sound weird, but I'm calling because you gave me your card at the Dolce & Gabbana boutique on Madison—"

"Ah, yes! The blonde!" She could hear the smile in his voice. "So, you have changed your mind about my taking your picture?"

"Maybe I could stop by your studio sometime soon . . . ?"

"How about tonight?" Kristof suggested.

Lilith smiled, pleased at how quickly the photographer had risen to the bait. "You mean that?"

"I never say things I don't mean. Unless I'm in love, of course," Kristof said with a laugh. "And even then, I wait until the third date. I am going to be very busy, starting tomorrow. If you want me to take your picture, it will have to be tonight or not at all."

"I think I can make it—I'll need to know where you are, though. All I have is your phone number."

"Very well," Kristof replied, and rattled off an address in Tribeca. "By the way, since you know my name, it is only fair that I know yours."

"My name is Lili—" Lilith was about to give her full name when she thought better of it and caught herself midway. If Kristof noticed her oddly clipped response, it did not register in his voice.

"I'll be here waiting for you, Lili."

Cally arrived just as the cleaners were locking up for the night. She quickly paid for the laundry, which was waiting for her in the collapsible shopping cart Sheila had dropped it off in the night before.

As she began pushing the heavily laden cart back to her apartment, she passed the remaining low-income six-story structures that had yet to be bought up and turned into overpriced lofts. Cally thought about how nice it would be to finally go out on the town for the sake of having a good time, not because she needed to roll drug dealers in order to pay the light bill or buy a new pair of shoes. Ideally, she would have preferred to go out clubbing with Peter, but that was impossible.

Suddenly a tall, gaunt male figure stepped out of a darkened doorway just ahead of her, blocking the path. Cally quickly recognized him as Johnny Muerto, one of her former schoolmates at Varney Hall—on those rare occasions he'd bothered to come to class.

"Looky what we got, boys," Muerto said with a nasty laugh, motioning to his half dozen followers, who emerged from the shadows to cut off Cally's escape. "What's the matter, oldie? You get lost on your way to Bloomingdale's?"

Muerto was scarecrow thin with a face that resembled a skull with skin stretched over it. An unruly shock of hair, as black and shiny as the feathers on a crow, hung down to his shoulders. Rumor had it that Muerto had personally driven stakes through the hearts of two old-ies who'd made the unfortunate choice of slumming on New Blood turf.

"What are you talking about, Johnny?" Cally asked. "I'm no oldie and you know it."

Muerto's lizard lips pulled back into something that was more snarl than smile, revealing yellowed fangs. "The grapevine has you attending Bathory Academy."

"And you *believe* that?" Cally retorted, trying to keep the fear out of her voice. Even though she was pretty good at hand-to-hand and could summon storms and lightning, there was no way she could take on all seven gang members at one time, and they knew it.

"Well, you certainly ain't hanging round like you used to. So what am I *supposed* to think?"

"I'm surprised you think at all."

"Ah. You hurt me, Cally." Muerto tapped his rib cage with one crooked, clawlike finger. "Really, you do."

While she was distracted, a shifty, rat-faced gang member reached out and snatched the laundry cart away from Cally.

"Keep your hands off my stuff, you creep!" she yelled as he dug through her belongings, tossing clothes in every direction.

"Muerto! Look at this!" he squealed, holding aloft a school blazer.

"Give that back!"

Cally tried to snatch the telltale jacket, only to have her arm grabbed.

Muerto pointed at the crest. "What's this? Looks like a big ol' *B*. Wonder what *that* stands for?"

"I *said* give it *back*, Johnny!" Cally shouted.

"Oh, I'll give it back to you," Muerto said. He twirled the jacket like a matador's cape, keeping it just outside her grasp. "But first you have to surrender that kiss you owe me."

Cally raised her right hand and an arc of electricity shot from her palm, striking the rat-faced gang member. Then she turned and fled.

"Don't just stand there!" Muerto shouted. *"Get her!"*

Cally ran as fast as she could, the gang cackling and screeching at her heels. She knew better than to scream for help. The families who lived in the shadows of the Williamsburg Bridge had learned long ago that it was safer to turn a deaf ear and a blind eye to those things that wandered their neighborhood after the sun went down.

Cally ducked between a couple of tagged-up old warehouses, but halfway down the alley she was driven to the ground by a pair of razor-sharp claws slamming deep into her back.

"Quick, tie her hands!" Muerto screeched, resuming his human form. "She can't call lightning if they're pinned behind her!"

Cally bit her lower lip as one of them planted a knee in her back and tied her hands together with a length of wire. Although her vampire heritage meant her broken ribs were already healing, the pain she felt was still very real.

Two gang members yanked her to her feet by her bound wrists, holding her between them.

"What a shame," Muerto sneered. "Like my mama

used to say: 'All that flapping, only to die within sight of the cave.'"

"If you're going to kill me, get it over with," Cally spat.

"*Kill* you? Is that what you think I want to do?" Muerto feigned indignant surprise. "All I ever wanted from you was a kiss. Just one little *kiss*!" Muerto's tongue flickered, tasting the air like a snake. "The first time I try, you punch me in the throat and knee me in the cojones! The second time you nearly fry me and then run away! Why? Am I so damn ugly to you? Or is it because you think you're so much better than me? Is that it?

"I could have been nice to you, Cally. *Very* nice. But now I'm about to be very nasty. And when I'm finished with your fine, oldie ass, my boys are going to be even *nastier*."

Suddenly the alley was awash in the blinding glare of xenon headlights. Muerto instinctively raised his stick-thin arms to cover his light-sensitive eyes. Cally could see the outline of a car blocking the alleyway behind the gang members.

"Let the girl go," the driver said, stepping out of the car. His voice was very deep, with a distinctly Mediterranean accent.

"You're on Impaler turf, asshole! Back off!" Muerto snarled.

The passenger climbed out of the car and spoke in a

voice as hard as steel. "He *said* leave the girl alone!"

"On whose orders?" Muerto hissed, flashing his fangs in defiance.

"Mine," the passenger said.

The driver reached inside the car and switched off the headlights, revealing two men dressed in the dark suits, black shirts, and crimson silk ties of the Strega.

The driver looked to be in his early thirties, with a huge head and hands the size of catchers' mitts. His passenger was considerably younger but carried himself with the confidence of a much older man.

A look of open fear crossed Muerto's face, and his sallow features grew even paler. "A thousand pardons, sir! I didn't realize it was you!"

"That much is evident, fool!" the younger man snapped. "Now do as I command and let the girl go! She's a friend of the family."

"Forgive us, sir! We had no idea!" Muerto pleaded as he freed Cally's hands.

"If I want to hear your voice, Muerto, I'll ask you a question. Now go fetch her belongings."

"Yes, sir! Right away, sir!"

"Now!"

As Cally watched Muerto and his gang screech in fear and instantly take wing, she was reminded of the flying monkeys from *The Wizard of Oz.*

"Are you all right, Miss Monture?" the younger man asked.

"I'm okay, I guess. But how do you know my name? Have we met before?"

"No. But I know who *you* are, Cally," the stranger said, flashing a warm smile. "After all, my sisters have done nothing but talk about you for the last few days."

"Your sisters—?"

Running his fingers through his excellent haircut, he straightened the lapels of his Armani suit. "Allow me to introduce myself: I am Faustus Maledetto. But you can call me Lucky. And this is my driver, Bava."

"*Maledetto?* Then you're Bella and Bette's—?"

"Older brother?" He laughed and nodded. "Yes, I am. I just happened to be about on business, as it were, when I saw your predicament."

"How did you know it was me?"

"I saw the lightning strike," he explained. "There are no other fledglings in the city who can do such a thing."

Cally lifted an eyebrow in surprise. "So your father's talked about me as well?"

"Of course," Lucky replied. "Ours is, after all, a family business."

There was a loud rattling sound and Cally turned to see Johnny Muerto trotting up the alley, pushing the laundry cart as fast as it could go.

"H-here's the clothes, sir!"

"Don't bring them to *me*, you moron! They belong to *her*!" Lucky said, winking at Cally.

"Sorry, sir," Muerto said sheepishly, turning to Cally. "I mean, I'm sorry, miss. I folded them as best I could—"

Lucky stepped forward and grabbed Muerto by the scruff of the neck. "Hear me, Muerto, for I have no intention of repeating myself on this matter: this girl is under protection of the Strega. If you, or one of your pathetic followers, so much as *look* in her direction again, I'll rip off your head, savvy?"

"Y-yes, sir," Muerto stammered.

"Good." Lucky shoved the gang leader aside, taking out a crimson silk handkerchief from his breast pocket to wipe his hands. "Now get out of my sight."

"Yes, sir." Muerto bowed as he backed his way down the alley. "You are most merciful, sir."

"I despise that little *scarafaggio*," Lucky spat as he watched Muerto scuttle back to his gang. "If it were up to me, I would have destroyed him." He turned to his driver and pointed at the laundry cart. "Bava, put Miss Monture's things in the trunk."

"Hey! What's going on?" Cally asked as Lucky's undead servant popped open the trunk of the Lexus.

"There's no need to be alarmed," Lucky assured her. "The *least* I can do is drive you home."

Cally was not sure whether she should accept Lucky's offer. Even though he was her friends' older brother, he was also one of the Strega and therefore a very dangerous man. Besides, she *did* have a boyfriend, even if she couldn't tell anyone he existed. Peter might not appreciate her taking rides from this handsome young guy.

Still, there was something about Lucky Maledetto that intrigued her. Cally glanced at her watch. She *was* running late and the man *did* just rescue her. Under such circumstances, it would be terribly rude to turn down his offer—wouldn't it?

"Here you are, safe at home," Lucky said, turning around to smile at Cally.

"Thanks for the ride, Lucky."

"It was nothing. It's good to finally put a face to a name. You're even prettier than my sisters said."

"Thanks." Cally could feel her cheeks turning pink. "I'm glad we met tonight, too, Lucky. I don't know what would have happened if you hadn't been there."

"I'm just glad I could be of some assistance, that's all. Speaking of which, doesn't your family have undead to handle errands, instead of placing you at risk?"

"It's hard to keep undead servants in a two-bedroom condo, I'm afraid."

"I'm sorry, that was insensitive of me," he apologized. "I forget that not everyone lives the lifestyle my family does, even those with Old Blood pedigrees. I can send Bava to help get your laundry to your apartment if you like."

"No! No! There's no need to do that," Cally replied

as she climbed out of the car. "You've done *more* than enough already. Please give my best to your family."

As she turned to go inside the building, Cally glanced up and saw the curtain covering her living room window suddenly drop back into place.

Oh, boy.

Her mother was waiting for her just inside the door. "*What* are you doing getting mixed up with the Strega?"

"You're *spying* on me, aren't you!" Cally replied angrily.

"It's not spying if I just happened to be looking out the window!" Sheila retorted. "And you *still* haven't told me what you were doing getting out of a car full of Strega goons."

"They weren't goons!" Cally replied. "At least, not all of them."

"That man I saw unloading our laundry from the trunk of the car—is that who you've been seeing?"

Cally rolled her eyes in disgust. "You've got to be *kidding*, right? Do you really think that's the kind of guy I'd go for? Besides, he's undead!"

"What about the one who waved at you? Who's that? Vinnie Maledetto's son?"

"So what if it was?" Cally said testily as she trundled the laundry cart down the hallway. "Lucky gave me a lift back home, that's *all*. He was just being nice because I go to school with his sisters."

"You hang out with Vinnie Maledetto's kids?" Sheila gasped, a stunned look on her face.

"Duh, *yeah*! They're my *friends*, Mom. Bella and Bette, remember? I went to Bergdorf's with them yesterday."

"You only told me their first names!" Sheila protested. "You *never* said they were Maledettos!"

"I didn't think it mattered," Cally grunted as she removed the folded laundry from the cart onto her bed. "Maybe if you paid half as much attention to me as you do to your stupid vampire movies, you'd know what was going on in my life!"

"*That's* who you've been sneaking off to see, isn't it?" Sheila said accusingly. "The Maledetto boy! Don't lie to me. I *know* it's true!"

Over the years Cally had learned that it was far easier to tell her mother whatever it was she wanted to hear rather than try to reason with her. On those rare occasions when her mother felt compelled to interfere in her life, she was like a terrier going after a rat. Better she believe a lie than know the truth.

"Okay!" Cally sighed. "Yes! I've been sneaking off to see Lucky Maledetto! *There!* Are you happy now?"

The look of consternation on Sheila's face was replaced by alarm. "Cally, you've got to promise me that you'll *never* see that boy again! And you have to stop being friends with his sisters, too! Vincent Maledetto is the sworn enemy of your father!" Sheila said. "There is a vendetta between your bloodlines!"

"Why should that matter to me?" Cally snapped. "I don't even know who my father really *is*!"

"Cally, you have to believe me! The Maledettos are nothing more than assassins and thieves!"

"That might be true," Cally replied, pulling herself free of her mother's grip. "But at least Vinnie Maledetto is actually *involved* in his kids' lives, okay? He *cares* about them! That's more than I can say about *my* dad— whoever the hell he is!"

"But your father—"

"My father can rot in hell for all I care!" Cally snapped. "If he doesn't want me to have anything to do with the Maledettos, he can get off his ass and tell me himself, face-to-face. Otherwise, he can go screw! Go back to your movie, Mom. I've got to get changed."

"But—"

"Get out of my room!"

Sheila flinched visibly and then scurried out of the room. Cally slammed the door after her.

Sheila crossed the hall into the master bedroom, locking the door behind her. She sat down on her bed and picked up the phone. In the nearly seventeen years since he had walked out on her to return to his wife, she had only called him one time: to inform him that Cally's grandmother was dead. All other contact had been initiated by him. They had agreed it was safer that way.

After five rings, a cultured British voice came on the line. It was his manservant, of course.

"Curtis? It's Sheila. Tell him we've got trouble."

CHAPTER FIVE

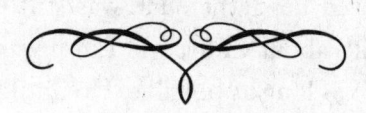

"There you are, princess!"

Lilith was on her way out when her father called her. "What is it, Dad?" she sighed.

Victor Todd took in the purple wool sheath dress with black-and-white patent leather trim and the red soles of the Louboutin pumps his daughter was wearing. "Very nice!" he said, nodding in approval. "Are you going out with Jules tonight?"

"I'm meeting him at the Belfry," Lilith said. It wasn't exactly a lie, but it wasn't the truth, either. She glanced at the Patek Philippe watch on her wrist. "Did you want to ask me something, Dad? Because I need to be somewhere and I'm running late. . . ."

"I just wanted to remind you that your mother is flying in from Monte Carlo for your debut at the Grand Ball. Her flight should arrive at JFK before dawn."

"Wonderful," Lilith groaned, far from thrilled by the news. "I can't wait."

She surveyed her father. He was still unaware she knew the truth about Cally, and Lilith wanted to keep it that way for as long as possible. Up until the moment she tasted her sister's blood, Lilith had been content to play the part chosen for her by her family. But now she knew her father had lied to her from the moment she was born, stringing her along with promises of power and privilege. She felt like some pathetic clot gulled into surrendering her blood in exchange for immortality, only to discover it included an eternity of servitude. It was only fair she get back at him by secretly rattling his cage, and it was easier for her to manipulate the situation if she didn't tip her hand. Besides, she enjoyed the feeling that came with knowing something her father did not know. It made her feel powerful.

"Oh, by the way, Dad, I almost forgot to mention it—but I had a bit of a run-in with the Maledetto twins yesterday."

Victor's smile disappeared. "Where?"

"Bergdorf's."

"Were they alone?"

Lilith shook her head. "Melinda and the New Blood were with them."

"*What* New Blood?" Victor frowned.

"You know, the stormgatherer I told you about," Lilith replied casually. "The one that got Tanith killed."

"This New Blood is associating with the Maledettos?"

Lilith had to fight to keep from giggling. Her father was trying *sooo* hard to make it look like he wasn't deliberately pumping her for information. Judging by the scowl on his face, he had been completely unaware of his little love child's taste in friends.

"They're thick as thieves. In fact, one of the Maledettos' drivers has been dropping the newbie off and picking her up from school."

"What could Vinnie Maledetto possibly want from this girl?" Victor mused aloud, his brow so deeply furrowed it looked like it was folded in on itself.

The head butler, Curtis, suddenly appeared in the doorway.

"Sorry to interrupt, Master, but there's an urgent call for you. It concerns the Williamsburg branch."

"Tell them I'll be right there." Victor turned back to Lilith, flashing her a wan smile. "Sorry, princess—I'm afraid I have some business I simply must attend to. I hope you enjoy yourself tonight."

"Don't worry, Dad." She smiled. "I already am."

The taxi smelled like ass, and the driver was so ugly he made an Orlock look good, but Lilith did not dare use the family chauffeur on her little jaunt to Tribeca.

As she rode up the elevator of the six-story brick warehouse that had been converted into loft space for stockbrokers, lawyers, and at least one fashion photographer, she could not resist using the stainless steel surface of the elevator doors to primp herself one last time.

"Welcome to my humble abode." Kristof smiled as he opened the door.

"Wow," Lilith said, staring up at the twenty-foot ceiling of the photographer's living room and work space. "I've never seen a loft where the person living in it also worked out of it!"

"You mean you've never been in a *real* loft before." Kristof chuckled as he helped her out of her black leather coat. "I was living here before Tribeca became trendy. The realtors basically had to do the conversion around me."

Lilith walked around the cavernous space full of backdrops, cameras, tripods, lighting stands, and photogenic umbrellas. She came to a stop in front of a wheeled wardrobe rack packed with costumes, hats, and other accessories.

"Do you do all your work here?" she asked.

"Only private shoots, like for friends or models who hire me to shoot their comp cards. You know, business cards," he explained on seeing the blank look in his guest's eyes. "So, tell me about yourself, Lili. . . ."

"Like what?" she asked as she pulled a feather boa off the rack and began arranging it around her neck.

"How about your last name, for starters?" Kristof

suggested, picking up one of his cameras.

"My *last* name?" Lilith froze, careful to keep her face turned so he couldn't see the panic in her eyes. She did not dare give him her real name. But she couldn't call herself Smith or Jones or something bogus like that. It had to sound authentic, but not so distinctive it could be easily traced. Suddenly it came to her. "It's Graves. Lili Graves." Surely Tanith wouldn't mind Lilith using her surname as a secret tribute.

"Pleased to make your acquaintance, Miss Graves," Kristof replied, snapping a shot of her with the feather boa draped about her shoulders. "Have you been photographed before?"

"Never."

Kristof obviously meant whether she had ever posed for a professional photographer before, but in this case Lilith was telling the honest truth. She was almost seventeen years old and there were no baby pictures, no vacation snapshots of her skiing in the Alps, no Polaroids of birthday parties, no home movies of her celebrating Long Night, the most important holiday of the vampire calendar. There was absolutely no photographic evidence of any kind to prove she ever existed. Nothing. Nada. Zilch.

"So, are you a student?"

"Yes."

"Hunter or NYU?"

He thinks I'm a college student! Lilith had to pull

the corners of her mouth down to keep from smiling. "Columbia, actually." She folded her arms, giving him a quizzical look, which he promptly snapped a picture of. "Have we started the shoot?"

"Not exactly," Kristof admitted. "How old are you? Eighteen? Nineteen?"

"Eighteen." It was another lie, of course, but what was one more on top of all the others?

"Are you new to the city?"

"No, I've lived here all my life—look, are you going to keep playing Twenty Questions?" she asked impatiently. "Because I'm *really* not comfortable telling you anything else about me right now. The only reason I called you is because I saw you with that model the other day. That's when I realized you were for real and not just some perv."

"I understand. You're a beautiful girl. It's a dangerous world. I'm sure you have strange men coming on to you all the time," Kristof said smoothly, a hint of admiration in his voice. "It's just that whenever I shoot someone I've never worked with before, I like to take a few casual shots to get a feel for how they move and hold themselves. The questions are a means of breaking the ice and getting familiar with you before I start shouting directions while shoving a honking-huge camera lens into your face. So . . . you were at the trunk show the other day? Funny, I did not see you there."

"I'm not surprised. You were utterly focused on that Gala bitch."

Kristof lowered his camera while raising an eyebrow. "You know her, then?"

"No," Lilith said quickly. "But I overheard her in the ladies' room, talking to a girl who asked her for modeling tips. She said some pretty mean things to her."

"Yes, well, the fashion world is *full* of divas, both in front of and behind the cameras." Kristof sighed. "Why don't we go ahead and get started for real?" He pointed to one corner of the loft, where a white backdrop stood in front of the exposed brick wall.

"So what do you want me to do?" Lilith asked.

"Just stand there for the time being until I get the lighting adjusted," he replied.

As the hot overhead light came on, Lilith instinctively raised a hand to shield her eyes. "Is that really necessary?" she asked.

"Only if you want to look like something other than a shadow. Besides, you have truly gorgeous hair and the most amazing eyes I've ever seen, and I want to properly highlight those features on film."

"You really mean that?" Lilith asked. Her threshold tolerance for flattery was so high that normally anything short of adoration failed to register on her ego. But there was something about Kristof that made even the slightest compliment feel like the highest of praise.

"Hold that feeling, whatever it is!" Kristof said

excitedly, bringing his camera back up. "Your face looks like it's glowing! It is *sooo* completely real!"

"Really?"

"I told you I never lie unless I'm in love—and even then, not until the third date!"

"You're terrible!" She giggled.

"That's it! Toss your head back—let me see that wonderful hair of yours fly!" Kristof reached over and switched on the fan next to him, aiming the airflow in such a way that it moved through Lilith's honey-blond locks like a gentle summer breeze. "Okay, Lili—I want you to imagine that there's an invisible thread pulling your head back and your chin up. No, higher. Higher. That's it! Stop! Perfect! Look at that long, beautiful neck!"

Lilith struck pose after pose, throwing her head back, shifting her weight between her hips, and striking asymmetrical stances, just like she'd seen the models do on Bravo and E! At first she felt kind of silly and self-conscious, but as Kristof shouted encouragement, she began to feel more and more confident.

"That's it, girl—work the boa! There we go—there's the shot! Beautiful! Rock the boa! There ya go! That's good! Now, I want you to keep playing with the boa while moving around—that's it! Keep shifting! Oh, yeah, I like that! Don't second-guess yourself, just go for it! Hold on a second, sweetie . . ." He sprinted over to the wardrobe rack and came back with a paper parasol.

"Here, I want you to swap out the boa for this."

"And do what?"

"Whatever you want—use your imagination!"

Lilith frowned for a moment, then opened the parasol and began to carefully walk heel over toe, pretending she was a circus acrobat up on the high wire in the center ring. She could almost smell the sawdust and make out the faces of the spellbound audience watching her from below.

"Perfect! Absolutely perfect," Kristof crowed, dropping down on one knee. "Okay, bring your face around to me but don't get caught doing it. Don't wrinkle your nose—keep your face relaxed. That's it!"

Normally Lilith despised it when others told her what to do, but when Kristof told her to move her arm or adjust her legs, she didn't mind in the least. In fact, she followed his instructions to the letter. For some reason, it seemed important to please him, even though she was at a loss to understand why.

As she finished her imaginary high-wire act with a curtsy to her audience, the opening bars to "Freeze Frame" suddenly broke the silence. Kristof reached into his pocket and pulled out a cell phone.

"Excuse me for a moment, will you?" he said apologetically. "I have to take this. Hello—?" The veins on the photographer's temples seemed to double in size as he listened to whoever was on the other end of the line. *"What?!?"* He looked up at the exposed beam ceiling in frustrated disbelief. "You're kidding me, right? When did it happen? Uh-huh. Is she okay? The doctors said *what*—? Well, no wonder she fell down the stairs! Karl, I've already booked the hair and makeup personnel and there's no getting the deposit back on the rental space for the shoot! You know the deadlines as well as I do. There's no way we can wait until she's ready and still make the cutoff dates. And finding another model on such short notice is going to be impossible. . . ." Kristof paused and glanced over his shoulder at Lilith, who was pretending she wasn't eavesdropping on his conversation.

"Is something wrong?" Lilith asked, trying to look as innocent as possible.

"Hold on a minute, Karl—I think I might have someone we can use. She's a brand-new face and a natural in front of the camera! Is she *pretty*? She's an absolute knockout! She doesn't have Gala's Malibu Barbie vibe, but she *is* classy. *Very* classy. How about we push back the shoot a day or so? I'll email you the pictures I've taken so far and you can decide whether you want to go with her or try and book another model through one of the agencies. Uh-huh. Great! I'll talk to you tomorrow, then."

Kristof slapped the cell phone shut and turned to grin at Lilith. "That was the U.S. rep for Maison d'Ombres. Guess what? Your pal Gala dropped some acid last night and ended up at the bottom of a flight of stairs. She's not going to be available for three months. Look, I realize that this is exceptionally short notice, not to mention a seriously *huge* leap—but I wasn't bullshitting when I told the rep you're a natural talent. Not only do you have the looks, Lili, you have the *fire*. I can see it in your eyes. You were *born* to be in front of the camera."

"You think I'm that good?" Lilith said, pretending to hesitate.

"Princess, you are so far beyond good it's *scary*! Just tell me you'll take the job, Lili."

"Okay, I'll do it."

She had originally intended to use her mesmeric abilities to beguile Kristof into offering her the modeling job, but it was nice to know that she didn't have to rely on blatant mind control in order to get what she wanted.

Lilith couldn't remember the last time she was so happy. The mixture of excitement and elation she was feeling was better than shopping, sex, and feeding combined. Not even looking in a mirror could compare to the rush that came from standing in front of a camera.

But the greatest thrill of all came from pretending she was no longer Lilith Todd, super-rich vampire debutante, but Lili Graves—a girl with no fixed history and no true past, but with a world of limitless possibilities before her. As Lili Graves she was free to be whatever she wanted to be—even a human.

How messed up was that?

"I'm going to go get myself a drink," Sergei announced. "Can I get either of you anything?"

Jules nodded and handed him a red-stained glass. "Yeah, another scotch."

"Anything for you, comrade." Sergei smiled crookedly.

Once Sergei was safely out of earshot, Carmen leaned across the divan, her green jersey halter dress providing Jules with an unobstructed view of her cleavage.

"I thought he'd *never* leave," she purred as she placed a hand on Jules's upper thigh. He shifted about uncomfortably but did not remove her hand from his leg. "I've been waiting for the right time to ask you this. . . ."

"Ask me what?"

"What do you think, silly?" Carmen replied coquettishly. "Do you want to escort me to the Grand Ball?"

"No." The answer was as bald and blunt as a billiard ball.

Carmen drew her hand back. The look on her face was one of utter disbelief. "*What* did you just say?"

"I said: 'no,' as in I do *not* want to escort you to the Grand Ball."

"But—I thought you *liked* me!" Carmen's voice

wavered, threatening to crack.

"I like *banging* you," Jules sneered. "Don't get the two confused, okay?"

Carmen got to her feet and hurried off. Jules heaved a sigh of relief.

"Where did Carmen go?" Sergei asked as he returned with the drinks.

"She went to the restroom," Jules said. "I think she's upset because I said I don't want to be her escort."

Sergei shook his head in disgust. "Chicks! There's no figuring them out—especially in *this* country! The girls here are too influenced by human media. The Founders had the right idea—it's better to keep a harem. That way you don't have to worry about one of them getting too much power over you."

"Are you insane?" Jules laughed. "If I had multiple brides, I'd be constantly breaking up catfights. I'd never get any peace!"

"Speaking of catfights: where *is* Lilith?" Sergei asked.

"She said she'd meet me at the club, but she didn't say when. She had some business to attend to first."

Sergei put aside his drink and scanned the room. "I was thinking of checking out this new VIP club I heard about from a friend of mine. You want to go?"

"Sure," Jules replied, a gleam in his eye. "What's it called?"

"The Viral Room."

"Let's take my limo," Jules said. "You got the address?"

Carmen returned from the ladies' room only to find Jules and Sergei gone. She hastily searched the dance floor, but there was no sign of them. As it sank in that she'd been ditched, Carmen began to hyperventilate, causing her bosom to heave.

A regulation hipster leaned over and tapped her on the shoulder. "Hey, lady—are you okay?"

Carmen instantly regained control of her breathing and smiled, twirling one of her red curls around her fingers. "I am *now*, lover."

Although the twentysomething in the designer jeans and ironic T-shirt didn't really look like Jules, even if she squinted, Carmen decided he would make a decent enough stand-in for her rage.

Her prey, being the complete and utter idiot most human males prove to be when an incredibly hot girl way out of their league shows any interest in them, was grinning from ear to ear.

The poor dope thought he was getting lucky.

CHAPTER SIX

The Viral Room was a two-level club in the trendy Meatpacking District. On their arrival, Jules and Sergei immediately made for the balcony lounge, which overlooked a large, square dance floor decorated with chaser lights.

"I like this place," Jules said as he scanned the room full of scantily clad women and giggly college girls. His eyes widened as he caught sight of a well-dressed young Asian man talking to an older African American man with dreadlocks hanging to his waist. "Whoa! Are those what I think they are?"

"They're weres, all right," Sergei agreed. "I think the younger dude's dad runs the were-tigers down in Chinatown. I don't know the were-lion."

As they spoke, the were-tiger turned to look up at the balcony. Although weres and vampires shared a distant ancestry, the relationship between the species was notoriously tense. The were-tiger studied the pair of fledgling vampires for a moment before returning to his conversation. Jules let out a sigh of relief and resumed his survey of the Viral Room's clientele.

"Whoa! Who's the hottie?" Sergei asked, nudging his friend.

Jules looked where Sergei was pointing and felt his heart begin to race. "That's the new girl at Bathory," he replied, trying to hide the excitement in his voice. The last time he'd seen Cally Monture, she'd been dressed in her gym suit and trying to sneak out of Ruthven's School for Boys. The moment he'd looked into her glittering green eyes, he'd found himself attracted to her. She was a fun tease.

"You mean she's one of us?"

"Not exactly." Jules shrugged. "She's a New Blood."

"Stand back, boy, and watch the master at work," Sergei leered. "I hear New Blood girls are easy and wild in the sack. Whoever gets to first base wins."

Cally looked around the crowded nightclub as she waited for Melinda to come back with their drinks. She was wearing the miniskirt she had been working on, made of black silk and embellished with scarlet flowers, a black long-sleeved turtleneck, and a pair of suede Marc Jacobs slouch boots she'd scored at a rummage sale. She felt a light tap on her shoulder. She turned to find a young man standing at her elbow. He had dark eyes and shoulder-length hair and was dressed in tight-fitting leather pants and a leather bomber jacket. He was holding a cell phone in one hand.

"Excuse me, miss. But there seems to be something wrong with my phone. . . ."

"Like what?"

"It doesn't have your number in it," he replied, flashing a smile that could melt the panties off the frostiest ice princess.

"Nice line, Romeo." Cally laughed. "Why don't you try it out on someone who's more your 'type,' huh? Maybe one of them?" She pointed to a table full of *Sex in the City* fangirls drinking muddled watermelon martinis and gossiping among themselves.

"I'm not looking to tap some clot, baby," the pickup artist said as he leaned forward to whisper into her ear: *"Ever make it with a real vampire before?"*

Cally recoiled, insulted. "I *beg* your pardon? What do you mean by 'real'?"

"You know," he said with a smirk. "Have you done it with an Old Blood?"

Suddenly a familiar face appeared over the pickup artist's shoulder. It was Lilith's boyfriend, Jules de Laval. Cally smiled, remembering their last encounter in the halls of Ruthven's.

"Is this man bothering you?" Jules asked.

"Definitely."

"You heard the lady, Sergei." Jules jerked his thumb over his shoulder in imitation of an umpire. "You struck out."

"No fair cock blocking!" Sergei growled under his breath.

"Oh? There are *rules*?" Jules stage-whispered in reply. "I must have missed that part. . . ."

"What are *you* doing here?" Cally asked.

"Not much—just checking the place out. Are you here by yourself?"

"No, I came with Melinda. She should be back any minute. . . ."

"You wouldn't happen to need an escort to the Grand Ball, would you?" Jules asked abruptly.

At first Cally laughed at the suggestion, but seeing the look in Jules's eyes, the smile on her face quickly disappeared. "Look, I don't want any more grief from Lilith. After the thing in the grotto—"

"What thing?" He frowned.

Cally gave him a puzzled look. "You don't know? Never mind. I just don't need the aggravation, that's all."

"Will you at least give me the pleasure of a dance?"

"I just told you I'm not looking to piss Lilith off."

"Lilith's not here, and I promise I won't tell her if you won't," Jules said with a mischievous smile.

Cally arched an eyebrow. "Okay—but just *one* dance."

"I promise," Jules said, taking her by the hand.

Suddenly Melinda was at Cally's side, tugging on her arm and glaring at Jules. "I need to powder my nose. Come with me."

"But—"

"Never mind that! Bathroom! *Now!*" With a single pull, Melinda freed Cally from Jules's grasp, dragging her down a crowded hallway and into the ladies' lounge.

"What do you think you're doing?" Melinda asked in exasperation as the door swung shut behind them.

"I was just going to dance with him, that's all," Cally assured her.

"Maybe that's all *you* were planning to do." Melinda looked around, checking to make sure no one could overhear them, and then leaned in close. "Look, Cally, I'm going to tell you straight up: you can't trust Jules. *No* woman can. The man's a dog. *Worse* than a dog: he's a wolf. And I'm not saying that just because he can turn *into* one! Jules's hobby is cheating on Lilith behind her back, *especially* with her friends. Bathory Academy is full of ex-BFFs that Jules has tagged."

"Did he ever hit on you?" Cally asked, unable to restrain her curiosity.

"Of course!" Melinda laughed. "But he didn't get anywhere. And don't let his good looks and the fact that he's nobility fool you—he's no Prince Charming.

When I shot him down, he started this rumor that I was a lesbian to get back at me. However, he *did* manage to seduce Carmen. Not that he had to try real hard with her. They've been screwing on the sly for the last couple of months."

"Ewwwww!"

"His family likes to pretend they're above this kind of stuff, but they desperately need the Todd bloodright if they want to survive this millennium. Since Jules can't dump Lilith, every time she does something that really pisses him off, he starts acting distant and makes a play for one of her friends. She freaks out, thinking she's losing him, and starts acting all submissive and girlfriendy and they make up. And then it starts *all* over again."

"But if Jules goes after Lilith's friends, why is he interested in me? I'm as far as you can get from being Lilith's BFF."

"If she gets that insecure when he's fooling around with her friends, imagine the drama if she found out Jules was fooling around with someone she *hates*."

"Well, I appreciate the heads-up on Jules, but you don't need to worry about me falling for his charms. Granted, he *is* super-hot, but I'm not interested. I've already got a boyfriend."

"Oh, really?" Melinda leaned in close, her eyes gleaming with excitement. "What's his name? Is he cute?"

Cally hesitated for a long moment, trying to decide whether to divulge any more than she already had. But as fearful as she was of exposure, she was eager for a chance to talk about Peter to someone else. "I can't tell you his name, because we're not supposed to be seeing each other. He's a little older than me, but he's really good-looking. He's so sweet and understands how I feel—"

"Does he go to Ruthven's?"

"No, you wouldn't know him," Cally said quickly. "He—he's from my old school." Cally paused, realizing she was saying too much about the wrong things. She needed to change the topic without triggering suspicion. "So who was the were-tiger I saw you talking to at the bar?"

Melinda's smile disappeared, and it suddenly occurred to Cally that she wasn't the only one whose love life could get her in big trouble. "*Please* don't tell anyone you saw us together, okay?"

"Don't worry, I won't." As she squeezed her friend's hand in assurance, Cally looked at her wristwatch and feigned surprise. "Is that the time? I need to get home! I still haven't finished recopying those passages for scrivening class. I'll see you at school, Melly."

Cally hurried out of the ladies' room and headed toward the door of the club. Just as she came within sight of the exit, Jules emerged from the crowd of sweaty, enthusiastic dancers, blocking her way.

"Leaving so soon?" he asked. "I can give you a ride if you like."

"That's okay—I can get back home on my own."

"Since you're leaving, can I see your cell phone for a second?"

"Why?" she asked as she handed the cell over to him. Jules did not answer but instead began to punch the keypad. "What are you doing?"

"Giving you my number," he explained. "That way, if you change your mind about my being your escort, you can call me." He smiled and handed her the phone. "There. It's done."

As Cally reached to take it back, Jules grabbed her outstretched hand and pulled her toward him, pressing his lips against hers. She tried to push herself away, but the heat of his mouth brought her even closer until their arms were wrapped around each other's waists. Then, as suddenly as it began, Jules broke off the kiss and, with a wink, darted back into the surging mass of bodies on the dance floor, leaving her with a hunger that had nothing to do with blood.

Cally walked out past the line waiting to get into the Viral Room, thinking about how Jules's kiss made her feel. Part of her wanted to turn around and go back into the club in search of him, but if she did that, then she would be just like her mother—and that was something

Cally had sworn she'd never let happen.

Jules was clearly big trouble: a ladies' man she couldn't trust, not to mention the future husband of her biggest enemy. Lilith had already attempted to kill her once before, simply because she'd seen him kiss her *hand*.

Still, as clearly wrong for her as he was, Cally had to admit she enjoyed Jules's company. He had a sense of humor and, in a lot of ways, came across as more fun to be with than Peter. Or at least that's how it seemed. Since she and Peter couldn't really go anywhere or do anything together outside the walls of Rest Haven Cemetery, it was hard to tell if she was being fair.

Cally stopped and shook her head. What was she thinking? How could she compare the two? What she and Peter shared was far deeper than the mere physical attraction she felt for Jules. Peter was the only person, besides her mother and grandmother, who knew what she really was. It didn't matter to Peter that she was half vampire or half human.

Even with diluted vampire blood in her veins, Cally knew she might live for centuries, which meant she had no choice but to watch the humans in her life grow old and die—including Peter.

Cally had loved her granny very much, and the thought of having to go through another profound loss such as that made her stomach knot up like a balloon animal. She wondered how humans could stand going through their lives watching those they cared for wither and die.

She could solve the problem of losing Peter simply enough by turning him undead—assuming a hybrid like her could even make undead in the first place. That way she could have him with her always, forever young and unchanging. But was that the right thing to do? What if whatever that attracted her to Peter, that made her love him, was no longer there after he became undead? What then?

Disturbed by the direction her thoughts were taking her, she suddenly found herself needing to hear Peter's voice. Maybe if she talked to him, the doubts that were plaguing her would disappear. She stepped off the sidewalk and into a nearby doorway and quickly dialed Peter's number.

One ring. Two rings. *Come on, Peter, answer.* Three rings. She felt a tiny rush of relief as the other line picked up and a familiar voice filled her ear.

"Hi . . ."

"Peter! Sorry I'm calling so late—"

"I can't take your call right now, but please leave a message."

Cally frowned and snapped the cell phone shut. Normally Peter always answered the phone, no matter what time she called. Before she could obsess any further over her boyfriend's late-night whereabouts, a shout of alarm broke the relative quiet.

Cally leaned out of the doorway where she was standing in time to see Melinda running in the direction of the river. Three figures pursued her—and they held crossbows at the ready.

As the strike team thundered across the decking of the recreation pier, the vampiress they were chasing whirled to face them, hissing in angry defiance. The trio of vampire hunters, composed of two men and a woman, automatically fanned out, crossbows cocked, effectively cutting their target off from the shore.

Their prey suddenly dropped onto all fours, transforming into a black panther in the amount of time it took the strike team's leader to yell, *"Shoot her!"*

Before any of the vampire hunters could fire their weapons, the panther leaped, sinking three-inch fangs into the team leader's throat. He shrieked in terror as she bore him to the deck of the pier.

"Drummer!" the female vampire hunter screamed, opening fire on the creature attacking her friend. Arrows from her five-shot repeating crossbow pistol pierced the panther's right flank and leg, causing her to yowl in agony and let go of the team leader's throat.

Before any more shots could be fired, there was a loud roar and a were-tiger leaped over Drummer's body, positioning itself between the vampire hunters and their quarry. The great cat snarled at the startled humans, then turned its gold-and-black flank to them, protecting the wounded panther with its own body.

"Sam, call for backup!" the younger man yelled, opening fire on the snarling were-tiger.

"Eagle's Nest, this is Strike Team Delta!" Samantha shouted into her wireless headset as she scrambled to reload her pistol crossbow. "Drummer's down! Repeat, Drummer's down! We need backup *immediately*! Over!"

Arrows tore through the were-tiger's rib cage and spleen. The big cat shrieked in agony, then collapsed heavily onto its side. The panther struggled to her feet and pressed a bloodied muzzle against the were-tiger's head. Although the huge were-cat was bleeding and in pain, it closed its burning yellow eyes and began to purr. The panther then raised its head and stared into the eyes of the young vampire hunter. As he drew a bead on the great cat's forehead, he suddenly found the pistol crossbow he was holding heavy, almost too heavy to hold up. He felt his grip on the handle of the weapon start to weaken. . . .

"Snap out of it!" Samantha yelled, pushing her dazed teammate aside. "She's trying to mesmerize you!" Before Samantha could fire her weapon, there was a smell of ozone in the air and all the hair on her arms and the back of her neck stood erect. Without warning, her entire body was in excruciating pain, as if a million red-hot needles had been suddenly thrust into every centimeter of her skin.

Peter Van Helsing stared in horror as his teammate collapsed onto the decking of the pier. He spun about, his finger on the trigger of his loaded crossbow, ready to send an arrow into the heart or brain of whatever was behind him. Then he froze. It was Cally, standing twenty feet away, a ball of pulsing electricity cupped in the palm of her hand.

The lovers stood staring into each other's eyes for what seemed like an eternity. Upon hearing the sound of beating wings, they looked up to see the silhouette of a large gargoyle rapidly approaching from across the river. It was Talus, Christopher Van Helsing's lethal pet, arriving in response to Samantha's SOS. Cally and Peter exchanged a quick glance, and Peter sent the crossbow arrow sailing over his girlfriend's shoulder. Cally hurled her fistful of lightning down the length of the pier, where it struck an ornamental stainless steel waterwheel, causing it to light up like a Fourth of July pinwheel.

Peter blinked, momentarily blinded by the flash, only to find Cally had disappeared. He knelt beside Drummer, but when he couldn't find a pulse, he moved on to Sam. She was alive—just barely. As he got back on his feet, he looked to where the vampiress and the

were-tiger had been. There was nothing there but a fistful of bloodied arrows and fur.

Lilith scowled as she impatiently swirled her AB neg
with bourbon around in its glass. Where in the name
of the Founders was everybody? She had arrived at the
Belfry fifteen minutes ago, expecting to meet everyone
in the Loft, but there was no sign of anyone. Just as she
was about to call Jules on her cell and ream him out for
standing her up, she spotted him coming up the stairs
from the dance floor.

"Where have you been? I've been looking all over for
you!" she scolded as he sat down beside her. "Did you
just get here?"

"Yes and no. I was here earlier, but I left to check out
this new VIP bar with Sergei."

"How was it?" she asked, mildly curious.

Jules shrugged. "I'm back, aren't I?"

"See anyone there worth talking about?"

"Nope," he lied. "Have you been waiting long?"

"Thirty minutes," Lilith lied in return, pushing her
lower lip out in a practiced pout. "I thought you'd forgotten me."

"Sorry for the trauma," Jules said with a crooked
smile, taking her hand in his. "So, what were you doing
earlier?"

"Shopping for a new gown for the Grand Ball. Mom

is cutting her vacation short so she can attend. Ugh." While the first part was a lie, the second was true enough.

Jules raised an eyebrow. He was all too familiar with Lilith's rocky relationship with her mother. "Irina's in town? For how long?"

"The rest of the Dark Season, I'm afraid." Lilith grimaced.

"Bummer," Jules agreed. "So, have you talked to your dad about going with me to Vail for Long Night?"

"I thought your father said you couldn't go to Vail unless you passed alchemy."

"Don't worry—it's in the bag." He laughed. "Exo's been helping me."

"By 'helping' do you mean he's tutoring you or that he's doing your homework for you?"

"He does it for me," Jules admitted sheepishly. "But I copy it down in my own handwriting once he's finished."

"Sweet!" Lilith exclaimed, her eyes lighting up. "I guess there *is* an upside to having a spod like Exo hanging around all the time."

"So, are you going to ask your dad about going on the ski trip with me?"

"I dunno . . ." she said hesitantly. "Dad usually wants the family together for Long Night. He's kind of Old World that way."

"If you ask him, he'll let you go. He *never* tells you no, Lili, and you know it! After all, you're the only daughter he's got. How could he deny you anything?"

"Cally! Thank goodness you're home! I was beginning to get worried."

Cally groaned at the sight of her mother standing in the foyer of their apartment, anxiously wringing her hands. It had been a hard night for her, and the last thing she needed was more of her mother's nuttiness.

"Mom, whatever you've got to say—I don't want to hear it," she said wearily, brushing past her. "I just want to get cleaned up and go to my room."

"Cally—you *can't* go to bed yet," Sheila said, grabbing her daughter's arm. "We have a visitor."

"We have a *what*?" Cally turned to look at her mother in disbelief. In the two years since they'd moved into the condo, no one—outside of the occasional delivery boy—had ever set foot inside their home.

"He's waiting for you in the living room," Sheila said gently, pointing to a well-dressed stranger seated on the chaise lounge.

As Cally entered the room, the stranger got to his feet to greet her. He was tall and well built and appeared to be in his mid- to late thirties, with dark hair going salt-and-pepper at the temples, brooding good looks, and an expressive mouth. But what caught Cally's attention were his eyes: they were the same color as her own.

"Hello, Cally." The stranger smiled, holding out his hand in greeting. "I'm glad to finally meet you. My name is Victor Todd. I'm your father."

CHAPTER SEVEN

Ever since she was a little girl, Cally had fantasized about this very moment, playing the meeting with her father over and over in her head each dawn as she lay in bed, waiting for sleep to come. In her fantasy, her father was a handsome, rich, and powerful vampire lord, kind of a cross between James Bond and Dracula.

For once, reality seemed to be keeping pace with her dreams.

Of all the possible candidates, Cally had never dared hope her father would turn out to be Victor Todd, the man responsible for single-handedly bringing the vampire race into the space age. It was like a human child discovering her biological father was Bill Gates. But if Victor Todd was her father, then that meant . . .

"Lilith is my sister?" Cally gasped. She felt her knees buckle and her head swim. She sat down on the chaise lounge, a dazed look on her face.

"Technically, she's your *demi*-sister," Victor said gently.

There were so many questions she wanted to ask him, but the only one she could think of was the one that hurt the most: "Why did you wait so long to tell me who you are?"

"I'm sorry I haven't come forward before now, Cally," Victor said earnestly as he sat down beside her. "But the truth of the matter is that when I left your mother to go back to my wife, I had no clue Sheila was pregnant. You *must* believe that. I did not even know you existed until after your grandmother died, when your mother finally contacted me."

Sheila nodded in agreement. "What your father says is true, Cally. Your grandmother didn't *want* Victor to know about you and did everything in her power to poison you against him. It's not that your father didn't care about you; he simply didn't know."

"But why didn't you tell me after Granny died?"

"It has everything to do with my wife." Victor sighed. "If Irina learned of your existence, she would not hesitate to kill you. As far as she's concerned, you are a threat."

"If you're so worried about your wife finding out

about me, why did you send me to Bathory Academy?" Cally frowned. "Lilith and I have been crossing swords since the moment I arrived!"

"The reason I sent you to Bathory is simple: to protect you."

"Protect me?" Cally asked. "From what?"

Victor shifted uneasily. "About a month ago, I received a tip from a mole planted within the Institute that their leader, Christopher Van Helsing, has been searching for you. He plans to use you in some insane plan of his to rid the world of vampires forever."

Cally's stomach flip-flopped on hearing the Van Helsing name. She averted her eyes, hoping her father would not notice her lack of surprise when he mentioned the Institute trying to track her down.

"Chris Van Helsing?" Sheila exclaimed, a startled look on her face. "Why is that nut job trying to find my little girl?"

"It's a very long and involved story, I'm afraid," Victor said. "The upshot is that, because Cally is the daughter of a vampire and the granddaughter of a witch, she may have inherited a rare vampire ability known as the Shadow Hand."

Cally frowned. "What's that?"

"It is a dangerous power that allows whoever wields it to kill anyone, vampire or human, simply by touching them. Pieter Van Helsing had it and used it to wreak havoc on our people on a level unlike any vampire hunter before him. Then in 1835 he destroyed the original Bathory Academy and Ruthven's School for Boys.

"When your grandfather, Adolphus, learned what had happened, he tracked the vampire killer down. Then he drained Van Helsing's blood, usurping his bloodright and powers."

"Did your father get the Shadow Hand next?" Cally asked.

Victor shook his head. "Nor did it manifest with me. When Lilith was born, I watched her closely. No again. As it turns out, *you* are the one who carries the Shadow Hand."

"That's *it*! I'm calling bullshit on this right now!" Cally said angrily. "How could I *possibly* have this Shadow thingy without knowing about it? I mean, I started developing stormgathering abilities when I was *thirteen*. Remember when I accidentally made it rain inside our old apartment?"

"Your grandmother was *so* mad you ruined her sofa." Sheila chuckled.

"See? There's no way I could have the kind of power you're talking about without it making itself known before now."

"I'm afraid it already has, Cally . . . you just didn't realize it." Victor handed her a piece of folded parchment he'd taken from the breast pocket of his suit. "I only recently received this from Madame Nerezza. It's a report by your physical education instructor, Coach Knorrig. Go ahead: read it. She describes a manifestation of the Shadow Hand while you were in a partial trance during your physical skills assessment. Do you remember that?"

"Yes. I remember." Cally nodded, her voice becoming distant as she tried to recall what had happened in the grotto that night. "I was trying to shapeshift into a wolf and something . . . something strange happened. I don't really know what."

"Neither did your physical education instructor—at least not fully. But your headmistress recognized the Shadow Hand when she read Knorrig's report. Luckily, Madame Nerezza is an old friend of the family: she's agreed to keep the information secret.

"However, I have reason to believe a member of the school staff leaked a copy of the report to Vinnie Maledetto. That is why he has suddenly expressed such a keen interest in your welfare. He hopes to win your trust in order to turn you into an assassin for the Strega."

"No! You've got it all wrong!" Cally shook her head in protest. "That's not the reason the Maledettos are nice to me. One of the twins got stuck with a bat face after flying class, and I helped her turn back. Vinnie—I mean, Mr. Maledetto—provided me with a driver to thank me for helping his daughter, that's *all*."

"What you say could very well be true. Perhaps it started innocently enough—but I can tell you that nothing involving Vinnie Maledetto stays innocent for long. The man has an unerring ability to identify the deadliest thing in a room and exploit it to his own ends. And you, my dear, are the deadliest by far. You cannot trust the Maledettos, Cally—not the father, not the son, not even the girls. Your mother told me of your involvement with Lucky Maledetto. . . ."

"My what?" Cally was momentarily baffled—she'd forgotten trying to throw her mother off Peter's scent by claiming she'd been sneaking off with Lucky.

"He and his kin are sworn enemies of all who carry Todd blood in their veins. That is why you must break your ties to that accursed family."

"But Bella and Bette are my *friends*!" Cally protested.

Seeing the look on his daughter's face, Victor placed a hand on her shoulder. "I understand how confusing all this is for you. I realize you must feel that I have no right to come in here and tell you who you should and shouldn't be friends with. I haven't been a father to you up to this point, Cally, but I want that to change." The serious look on Victor's face lightened as he moved his hand to touch her chin, tilting Cally's head back so that she looked directly into his eyes. "I've seen your grades and read all the summaries your instructors have written about you. You are an incredibly intelligent and gifted girl, with or without the Shadow Hand, and one I am proud to have as my daughter. I pray to the Founders that you will find it in your heart to forgive me for whatever hurt my actions may have caused you over the years. Still, you *must* believe me when I tell you that severing your ties with the Maledettos is for your own good."

Cally took a deep breath and stepped back as she pondered what to do. She had visualized all sorts of scenarios for when she finally met her father face-to-face. Some were angry. Others were tearful. Some were bittersweet. But not one of them had involved him asking her to discard her friends in the name of family.

Part of her wanted to tell him to forget it. She had gotten along just fine without him up to now. But what if she told him no and he decided to wash his hands of her entirely and she never got to see him again? She had spent her entire life waiting for her father to make his appearance. She wasn't about to risk his leaving her again.

"Okay, I'll do as you say," she sighed.

Her father smiled and opened his arms. Cally stepped into his embrace, rubbing her cheek against the lapel of his wool suit as he hugged her. "That's my girl," Victor Todd said, smiling in quiet triumph as he stroked his daughter's hair. "That's Daddy's girl."

Cally closed her eyes and sighed happily to herself. He even *smelled* like she had imagined fathers should.

CHAPTER EIGHT

A s Lilith hurried down to the bottom floor of her family's penthouse apartment in time for her waking meal, she was unpleasantly surprised to find her mother already waiting for her in the dining room.

"Hello, Lilith," Irina Viesczy-Todd said, glancing up from her crossword puzzle just long enough to acknowledge her daughter's arrival. Mother and child had not seen each other in six weeks, which was just fine with all concerned.

Irina held a cut-crystal goblet filled with scarlet liquid in one hand, and the mechanical pencil she used on her crossword puzzles was in the other. With her strong cheekbones and long blond hair artfully piled atop her head, Irina looked to be in her early thirties rather than the 150 years Lilith knew her to be. As Lilith drew closer, she noticed her mother was still dressed in her satin robe, which revealed far more toned and artificially tanned flesh than any daughter wanted to see.

"Hello, Mother," Lilith said sullenly.

"You needn't sound so put upon," Irina said as she sipped at her waking repast, which had been triple-screened for impurities and contaminants such as HIV, West Nile virus, and hepatitis. "What kind of mother would I be if I wasn't present for my only daughter's Grand Ball debut? By the way, while I was at the tables in Monaco, I received a letter from an old school friend of mine—Verbena Mulciber."

"You mean Madame Mulciber?" Lilith looked up, surprised. "My alchemy teacher?"

Irina nodded. "She wrote to inform me that you're on the verge of flunking out."

"It's been difficult for me to focus on schoolwork lately, what with Tanith being killed and everything," Lilith replied. Suddenly an undead servant in a maid's uniform appeared, took the crystal goblet from Lilith's place setting, and vanished into the kitchen to fill it with warmed blood.

"You fledglings today have no idea how easy you have it! By the time I was your age, half of my graduating class had been annihilated," Irina said, clucking her tongue in disapproval. "If I'd let my friends being killed interfere with my education, I'd still be in Russia, tapping peasants on some hell-forsaken communal farm! Bathory Academy has one of the finest preparatory programs available *anywhere* for girls your age, and since your great-aunt Morella founded the school, the *least* you could do is not embarrass the family by getting kicked out."

Irritated by her mother's needling, Lilith countered, "If their prep program is so good, then why did they enroll a New Blood?"

"New Blood?" Irina looked up from her crossword, her eyes darting around the room as if there might be ninjas hiding in the corners. "There is a New Blood attending Bathory?"

"Her name's Cally," Lilith said, fighting back a smile as she dangled Daddy's secret daughter in front of her unwitting mother.

"The very idea!" Irina exclaimed, her eyes flashing. "I will have your father speak with the headmistress about this outrage. We are *not* paying for you to rub elbows with a bunch of ne'er-do-wells!"

"I'm glad you feel that way," Lilith said as the maid returned with the goblet full of warmed blood. She turned to glare at the servant. "Hey! What are you, *stupid* or something? Get me a straw! I don't want to screw up my lip gloss before I get to school!"

The maid jumped like she'd been stuck with a hot poker, a look of genuine alarm in her eyes. "Yes, Miss Lilith! I'm so sorry! Right this minute!"

Within seconds a straw was bobbing in the goblet. Lilith took a tentative sip. AB poz, with just a trace of anticoagulant to keep it free flowing: not a bad way to start off the night.

"There's no other way I *could* feel about something like that," Irina replied flatly. "However, that is no excuse for your abysmal performance at school. Your father and I expect to see significant improvement in your grades after the Grand Ball, young lady! You're spending far too much time partying and not enough studying." Irina's tone was even but firm, an unmistakable warning that she was in no mood for one of her daughter's tantrums. "Now why don't you see if Bruno has brought the car around for you, my dear?"

Lilith snatched up her book bag and headed out the door for school. As she rode the elevator down to the lobby, she began to think that maybe having Irina home for the holidays might not be that horrid after all. Imagine all the near collisions she could orchestrate between Cally and her mother! If nothing else, watching her father scramble to prevent Irina from learning his dirty little secret would be deeply satisfying.

As Cally entered Madame Boucher's Avoiding Detection 101, she spotted Lilith seated in one of the desks, gossiping with Carmen. What she now knew about Carmen and Jules made her blush, and she quickly looked away. She saw Bella Maledetto sitting near the back, waving at her and pointing at the open desk across the aisle. Without thinking, Cally took an automatic step in the direction of her friend, only to remember the promise she had made to her father the night before to disconnect herself from the Maledetto family.

Instead of sitting down next to Bella, Cally slid into the desk beside Annabelle Usher. She guiltily glanced over at her friend and saw a look of baffled hurt on Bella's face. Cally sighed and turned away. Tonight was the start of what would probably be a very difficult and lonely time in her life, but she told herself it was worth proving her loyalty to her father and winning his approval.

"Good evening, young ladies," Madame Boucher said as she looked out across her class. She was a small-boned woman who appeared to be in her early fifties, her ginger-colored hair piled high atop her head in an old-fashioned beehive.

"We've studied some of the tried-and-true methods of avoiding detection, such as faking your own death and later reappearing in the same community as a younger relative, preferably a niece or granddaughter.

"Today we'll start focusing on practical camouflage and misdirection. I will be drilling you on these techniques until they become as natural to you as breathing or flying.

"When I was a schoolgirl, avoiding detection wasn't as necessary a skill as it is today. Back then, reflective surfaces were nowhere as common as they are today.

Everything was made out of wood and stone, not plate glass and stainless steel!"

The instructor motioned to an undead servant dressed in the school's livery, who pushed a dolly carrying a large, upright object covered by a drop cloth to the front of the class.

"Ladies, it is time that you get to know your enemy!" Madame Boucher said as she yanked the cloth away, revealing a full-length cheval mirror. An audible gasp rose from the assembled students. A couple even hissed and instinctively raised their arms to shield their faces.

Since she had been raised around mirrors, Cally's reaction to the looking glass was far more muted. She glanced around and noticed that the only other student in the room who didn't seem agitated was Lilith.

"There's no need to be afraid," Madame Boucher assured her class as she stepped in front of the mirror. Or at least her clothes did. Her gray tweed skirt, white silk blouse, and maroon cardigan appeared to hang empty in midair.

"The most common form of camouflage is the creative use of clothing, in particular hooded cloaks, as well as using the humans' own numbers against them. After all, who would notice one reflection missing from the hundreds half glimpsed at any one time in the windows along Sixth Avenue?

"First, you must become familiar with your reflections so that you understand what the humans do and don't see in a mirror. How many of you have *never* seen yourselves in a mirror before?"

Annabelle Usher raised a trembling hand.

"Big surprise there, Usher! Not!" Lilith snickered.

Annabelle was the last of a once-fabled line who had fallen on such hard times she did not have a dresser to see to her appearance before leaving the house. As a result, the poor girl usually came to school looking like a Barbie doll that had fallen into the hands of a sadistic little brother.

"Like ballet, you cannot master camouflage unless you can *see* what you're doing wrong. I want each and every one of you to line up and step in front of the cheval and look at yourself first full face, then profile, and then over your shoulder. And, Miss Usher, I want *you* to be the first in line."

The students got out of their desks and formed a single line, with Annabelle serving as its reluctant head. When she stepped up to the mirror, her gaze was firmly fixed on her shoes instead of on the silvered glass in front of her.

"Go ahead and look at yourself, Annabelle," Madame Boucher said gently. "There's nothing to fear."

Annabelle hesitantly raised her eyes, slowly tracking up her legs and torso until she reached her face. She stared for a long moment at her crudely drawn eyebrows and the clownlike splotches of rouge on her cheeks, then dashed from the room in tears.

"Can you believe that spod didn't know how horrible she looks?" Lilith snickered as she stepped up to take Annabelle's place in front of the mirror. Instead of flinching or cringing at the sight of her reflection, Lilith casually flipped the hair out of her face.

"Excellent form, Lilith," Madame Boucher said approvingly. "Very confident and self-assured."

As she watched her sister turn away from the mirror, Cally found herself feeling bad for all the mean things she'd said and thought about Lilith—not to mention kissing her boyfriend at the Viral Room last night. They *were* siblings, after all. Even if Lilith didn't know that was the case, *she* did, and she had been raised to honor family ties.

"Nice job, Lilith," Cally said as she walked back to her desk.

Lilith turned and glared at Cally as if she'd just hocked a loogie at the side of her head. "*What* do you mean by that, New Blood?"

"I was just trying to compliment you on how you handled yourself in front of the mirror, that's all. You did it like a pro."

"Are you insinuating that I *like* to look at myself?" Lilith hissed, her blue eyes flashing.

"No, I was just being nice, Lilith."

"Brownnosing is more like it," Lilith spat. "What

are you trying to pull, Monture?"

"Miss Todd! Miss Monture! *What's* going on here?" Madame Boucher asked as she moved to separate the two girls.

"She said I was a mirror junkie!"

"I said no such thing! She's lying!" Cally protested.

"Miss Monture, I will not tolerate you insulting others in my class!" Madame Boucher said sternly.

"But—"

"Not another word, Miss Monture!" Madame Boucher's beehive hairdo jiggled wildly atop her head as she wagged a finger in Cally's face. "I do not tolerate troublemakers, is that understood?"

"Yes, Madame Boucher," Cally said, biting her tongue and dropping her eyes in deference.

"What else can you expect from someone like her?" Lilith sneered. "Her mother's a slut."

Without any warning, lightning leaped from Cally's left hand, and for a fleeting second she was tempted to let it strike Lilith. Instead, she snapped her hand back, like a cowboy cracking a bullwhip, and sent the deadly charge arcing in the opposite direction.

The other girls standing in line scattered, screaming in terror, as the lightning bolt flew past them and struck the mirror, shattering it to bits.

"My mirror!" Madame Boucher wailed in disbelief. "Do you realize what you've done, you wretched child?! That was an original Chippendale!"

"I'm sorry, Madame Boucher!" Cally said as she stared at the smoldering remains. "It was an accident. Honest! I didn't mean for *any* of this to happen!"

Madame Boucher went to her desk and furiously scribbled a note on a piece of parchment, handing it to the servant who had wheeled the now-demolished mirror to the front of the classroom. "Get *out* of my class, Monture! Gustav! Escort her upstairs and give this note to the headmistress. And send the second-floor janitor to come sweep this mess up while you're at it."

"As you command, Madame," Gustav replied, taking Cally by the arm. His grip was not rough, but neither could it be easily broken. "Come, young mistress," he said. "You must go to the office."

As she was led out of the room, Cally glanced over her shoulder and saw Carmen, Lula, and Armida clustered about Lilith, whose glossy pink lips were twisted into a triumphant smirk.

The headmistress sat behind her desk, dressed in a neat single-breasted gray tweed skirt suit with black velvet trim. She glanced up from the note Madame Boucher had written to look at Cally, who stood before her desk, hands clasped behind her back.

"As you well know, Bathory Academy is a vendetta-free zone," Madame Nerezza said sternly. "It is strictly forbidden for students to use their powers against one another in class."

"Yes, ma'am, I know that. And I'm *really* sorry about what happened, Madame Nerezza," Cally said earnestly. "I told Madame Boucher I didn't mean to do it. It's just that Lilith said something to me that . . . well, it made me lose my temper, and I reacted without thinking. I managed to keep the lightning from hitting anyone. . . ."

"Be that as it may, what you did is still grounds for permanent suspension."

"I'm being expelled?"

"No, child." Madame Nerezza sighed, shaking her head. "It would be negligent of me to do such a thing. You must be taught how to control the power you have.

"However, if you are to remain at Bathory Academy, you have to promise me that you won't let others provoke you again. The consequences could be disastrous for everyone involved."

"Yes, ma'am, I understand," Cally said. "Thank you for giving me a second chance."

"Something tells me that it would be best to give Madame Boucher time to cool down," the headmistress said with a smile. "Here's a pass to the scrivenery. Stay there until it's time for your next class."

"Thank you, Madame Nerezza."

"Before you go, I want you to have this as well." The headmistress handed Cally a sealed envelope. "It's Tanith Graves's invitation to the Grand Ball. Or it would have been had she not been killed. The presentation committee decided I should award it to the Bathory student most worthy of the honor. I was going to have it delivered to your home, but seeing that you're here, I thought I would give it to you personally. I realize it's on short notice. . . ."

"I'm flattered, Madame Nerezza, but you know I can't accept this," Cally protested. "I'm not entitled. I'm not a real Old Blood. And I'm half human."

"All the more reason for you to go, if you ask me," the headmistress replied. "With every decade, each technological advance, the world grows smaller and smaller. If vampires are to survive, we must come to terms with the human race. In you I see a glimmer of hope for our people's future. Besides, where's the harm? Go, have a good time. After all, Rauhnacht is for the young."

CHAPTER NINE

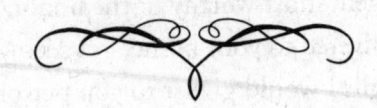

As Lilith exited the red double doors of Bathory Academy and climbed into the back of the waiting Rolls-Royce, she pulled out her iPhone and checked her messages. There were six voice mails waiting, all from Kristof. She instantly hit callback while pushing the button that raised the privacy screen between her and the driver.

"I've been trying to reach you all evening! Where have you been?" the photographer asked in an exasperated voice, not even bothering to say hello.

"I'm, um, taking night-school courses, and I have to keep my cell switched off while I'm in class." While her explanation was closer to the truth than anything else she'd told him so far, it was still a lie.

"Great news! Karl saw the frames I took last night

and decided you're perfect for the Maison d'Ombres launch! So you need to get your sexy butt to the location by nine tomorrow morning. I'm going to text you the address. But first, I want to make sure you get a good night's sleep, okay? You don't want to look like you've been up all night when you're in front of the cameras. Oh, and don't bother putting on your face beforehand, either. Stylists will be there to handle your makeup and hair."

"Do you think this is a good idea, Kristof?" Lilith asked, making sure her voice had just the right amount of girlish quaver.

"Kid, it's the best idea I've *ever* had! Tomorrow's going to be all kinds of crazy, but you have nothing to worry about. Just leave everything up to me."

Lilith smiled as she hung up. So far everything was going perfectly. Aside from pushing that bitch Gala down the stairs, she really hadn't had to cheat all that much in order to get her way. Still, it was frustrating not being able to talk to anyone about what was going on in her life.

After all, what was the point of being a fashion model if you couldn't brag to everyone you know and make them jealous?

"I brought new flowers, Granny," Cally said as she removed the withered bouquet from the memorial vase and replaced it with a fresh one. Her head was buzzing from all the stuff that had happened in the last twenty-four hours, and tending her grandparents' grave helped organize her thoughts.

She found herself thinking about the attack on the pier the night before. She'd been so focused on saving Melinda, it had never crossed her mind that Peter might be one of the strike team. She had been so close, so terribly, terribly close to firing raw lightning into his back. Praise to the Founders she stopped herself in time, but what if she hadn't? What if she'd accidentally killed him? The thought made her chest tighten up. Maybe it was all the stress and emotional turmoil from the last few days that had made her lose control and nearly fry Lilith in class.

It was times like these that she sorely missed Granny's wisdom. Sina Monture had worked hard to give Cally as normal a childhood as any kid with a vampire for a dad, an alcoholic for a mom, and a witch for a grandma could possibly hope for. Even though her grandmother would not have approved of the decisions she'd made or the individuals she was involved with, Cally had no doubt Granny still would have known exactly how to make things better.

Cally opened the invitation Madame Nerezza had given her and read the formal chthonic inscription. Cally could easily see that her name was in a different scrivener's hand than the rest of the invitation.

The Presentation Committee requests the honor of

presenting Miss Cally Monture at their three hundred and eighty-third annual Grand Ball this coming Rauhnacht, on the stroke of midnight. At the pleasure of the Count and Countess Orlock, King's Stone, East Hampton, Long Island, New York.

Initially Cally had been excited about being invited to the Grand Ball, but now that the thrill was starting to wear off, she wondered how she was going to actually be able to attend.

There were three things a vampire debutante had to have to be presented at the Grand Ball: a full-length black evening gown, an escort, and a father. She had already started work on a dress, but the escort and the father were going to be considerably harder to come by.

Cally had imagined that discovering her father's true identity would solve all her problems. But as it turned out, knowing who he really was could generate more trouble than not knowing. Cally wasn't sure which would be worse, her father discovering that she was secretly involved with a Van Helsing, or Peter finding out that she was really a Todd. Either one, she got the dirty end of the stick.

And there was no way Victor Todd was going to stand up in front of Old Blood society and openly acknowledge her as his daughter, especially with his wife and Lilith in the audience.

Suddenly there was a hand on her shoulder. Cally jumped like a startled cat, making a flawless two-point landing on her grandparents' headstone, her fangs bared as she hissed at the intruder.

"Calm down, Cally!" Peter said with a nervous laugh. "It's just me!"

Cally frowned. "What are *you* doing here?"

"I'm sorry; I didn't mean to scare you. I know we weren't supposed to see each other tonight, but after what happened at the pier, I wanted to make sure you were okay. . . ."

"I'm all right," she said as she hopped down off the tombstone. "It's just that after last night, I'm kind of jumpy."

"That's an understatement." Peter chuckled. His smile disappeared when Cally did not join in on his laugh. "Is something wrong?"

Cally didn't want to have to admit that she had come to Rest Haven so she could be alone with her thoughts. "I just wasn't expecting you, that's all," she said, trying to hide the annoyance in her voice.

"What's the matter?" He frowned. "You're acting like you aren't glad to see me."

"It's not that, Peter. It's just that, well, it was kind of weird seeing you trying to kill my friend."

"Cally, you know what I am, what I do."

"I know that; it's just that I never thought you would end up attacking anyone I know. Why didn't you tell me you were going to be there?"

"It never occurred to me you would show up at the

Viral Room. It was Drummer's decision to keep the club under observation."

"Who's Drummer?"

"He is, I mean, he *was* the strike team leader. We were stationed in a panel van parked on the street across from the club. Drummer recognized the girl we ended up chasing as a sucker. . . ."

"A *what*?" Cally said angrily, her eyes flashing.

"Sorry, I mean a vampire," Peter said, hastily correcting himself. "He's the one who made the decision to pursue her. Samantha and I were just following orders."

"Who's Samantha?"

"She's the woman you *fried*, Cally!" Peter replied testily. "Doc Willoughby says she'll need a couple of skin grafts for her back."

"I don't care," Cally retorted. "She was trying to kill Melinda!"

"So she and Drummer deserved what they got?"

"Yes! I mean, no!" Cally covered her face with her hands. No matter what she said, it seemed to be the wrong thing. She wasn't ready to talk about any of this yet. "I don't know what I mean, Peter. I'm just so confused. . . ."

"Cally, what's wrong with you?" Peter asked, a worried frown on his face. "We've never talked to each other like this before. It's not just what happened on the pier, is it?"

"I'm sorry if I'm acting really weird right now, Peter."

She sighed wearily. "It's just that I've had a *lot* to deal with in the last twenty-four hours, and it's really been messing with my head."

"What kind of stuff?"

"I don't want to say."

Peter smiled and stroked her hair. "C'mon, you can tell me," he said. "You said yourself that I was the only person you could really talk to."

"Not this time," she said, stepping away from him.

Peter took her firmly by the shoulder and turned her back around so that they were face-to-face. He gently lifted her chin so that he was looking directly into her sparkling green eyes. "I hate seeing you this worried. Please tell me what's wrong."

"Nothing's wrong, really. It's just that things are— complicated right now. Last night, after I got home from the pier, I found my father waiting for me in the living room."

"You're joking, right?" Peter's eyes were wide with surprise.

"Afraid not," Cally sighed. "I want to tell you who he is, but I don't think that would be a good idea right now. If it's okay with you, I'd rather wait until I figure out who I really am and where I fit in all of this."

"What's to figure out?" Peter smiled reassuringly. "You and I belong together. That's all that really matters, right?" He stepped forward, opening his arms to hug her, only to have Cally quickly sidestep his embrace.

"That's what I thought, too, but now I'm not so sure."

"What do you mean?" Peter asked, his smile sliding off his face like eggs off a plate. "You don't want to break up with me, do you?"

"Damn it, I don't know, Peter. All of this is so *confusing*! I still want to be with you, but I don't know how much longer we can keep seeing each other before something bad happens."

"What is there to be afraid of?" Peter asked, an edge of resentment in his voice.

"What is there *not* to be afraid of?" Cally replied with a humorless laugh.

"I don't understand." Peter frowned. "You've always said that our being together was worth the risks we have to take. What's made you change your mind?"

"I won't lie to you—what happened on the pier last night really made me rethink what we're doing. We almost *killed* each other."

"Yeah, but we *didn't*."

"That's not the point! I don't want to be in a position where we resent each other, Peter. And when you were talking about your friends, I could see it in your eyes, if only for a moment. You hated me for what happened to them."

Peter dropped his gaze. "It wasn't your fault, Cally. You didn't know it was me. You were just trying to help your friend."

"Peter—you don't understand. Even if I *had* known it was you beforehand, I still would have done the same thing. Just as *you* would have, even if you'd known Melinda was my friend. It's hardwired into us. And even though I know that you were just doing what you've been raised to do, part of me is still angry at you for attacking Melly, and, I'll admit, I'm also a little bit scared of you. I saw the look in your eyes when you spun around. You hated me right then as much as anyone can hate anything—up until you recognized me. Hate like that doesn't just go away, Peter. You and I both know that.

"I was dreaming we could run away somewhere and start a new life together, but the best we can ever hope for are stolen moments, nothing more. There's no future in this. Not for me, and certainly not for you. That's why I don't want what we have to be ruined any further."

As she moved to leave, Peter grabbed Cally's arm. "Don't do this, Cally!" he pleaded. "We can get it to work, I know we can!"

"Don't make this any harder than it already is, Peter."

"No. I *won't* let you do this to us!" he said, tightening

his grip. "I love you, Cally. Why are you tearing us apart?"

Suddenly her hand was on his throat, her fingers biting deep into the flesh. Peter let go of Cally's arm and began clawing at his neck, gasping desperately for air.

"Can't you see?" Cally whispered hoarsely as the tears ran down her face. "Love will *always* tear us apart."

Peter awoke to find himself sprawled across a grave. As he struggled to stand, his body was racked by heaving coughs that made his bruised throat burn.

He'd loved Cally with all his soul, and she had repaid him by crushing his heart and physically attacking him. His father was right: you couldn't trust vampires. Not even the half-human ones. They corrupted everything and everyone they came in contact with, including him.

He'd lied to his father about Cally's whereabouts, even tampered with evidence that might lead his father to her. And for what? He dared not tell his father what had happened for fear of losing his respect. And if the others at the Institute learned he'd covered for the sucker responsible for what happened to Big Ike, Sam, and Drummer, no one would be willing to partner with him ever again.

If only there was some way he could redeem himself. Maybe then he could close his eyes at night and not hear Drummer's screams. . . .

As he shuffled through the carpet of fallen leaves that covered the ground, Peter's eye was caught by what looked to be an envelope lying at the foot of a grave. On picking it up, a formal RSVP card fell out. It was written in some arcane alphabet. Frowning, Peter turned the envelope over and was surprised to see a computer-printed label, the address written in English, on the front. His eyes widened in surprise on spying the name Orlock.

While vampires liked to hold themselves above the lowly humans on whom they preyed, they apparently didn't consider it beneath them to make use of human inventions, such as the postal service. They would end up paying dearly for their carelessness.

CHAPTER TEN

neaking out of the house to go to the Maison
d'Ombres shoot turned out to be far easier than
Lilith had expected. Shortly before sunrise her parents bade each other good day and quickly retreated to
their separate suites. Within minutes of their master
and mistress retiring, the Todd family's undead staff
followed suit, shuffling off to the storage closets on
each floor of the penthouse, where they would spend
the coming daylight hours stacked on narrow shelves
like cordwood.

With the undead servants out of the way, that just
left the day shift, which consisted of the human thralls
who served as the Balmoral building's concierge, its
doorman, and the daylight drivers and other errand
runners. All Lilith had to do to sneak past them was to
walk out of the Balmoral via the loading dock instead

of the front door and hail a cab instead of calling for one of the family cars. It was just that simple and oh so exciting.

The shoot was being held at a full-service facility for New York's fashion and film industry, on West Thirty-fifth, in what was once the city's infamous Hell's Kitchen. As she entered the ground-floor studio, Lilith was surprised to find herself standing in what looked like a movie soundstage. In the middle of the twenty-five-hundred-square-foot room was a replica of a Parisian garret—or at least three quarters of one—complete with a window that looked out onto the Eiffel Tower. The studio was full of lighting techs, carpenters, and other less identifiable people, all of them clutching clipboards in one hand and cups of Starbucks coffee in the other as they spoke frantically into their Bluetooth headsets.

"*Lili!*"

Kristof trotted toward her from the other side of the studio, a smile on his face. He was accompanied by a wiry man with dramatically highlighted hair. "You're right on time!"

"My God, Kristof! She's absolutely *stunning*!" the other man gasped, putting his hands to his mouth in an exaggerated show of surprise. "Where on *earth* did you find her?"

"D&G, believe it or not," Kristof replied with a laugh. "Lili, I would like you to meet Tomás, the art director for today's shoot. I've got to set up a few more lights, so I'll be leaving you in his very capable hands."

"Let's get you in the makeup chair!" Tomás said, taking Lilith by the arm. "So, Kristof tells me you're a virgin."

"*What?*" Lilith's cheeks colored slightly.

"Not in that sense of the word, sweetie." Tomás laughed. "If anyone else but Kristof had told me that he was using someone with absolutely no professional modeling background to launch a new fashion line, I would have laughed in his face. But if there is one thing I *know*, it's that Kristof is never wrong when it comes to talent. And if he says you can pull this off, then I have the utmost faith in his decision."

The makeup and hair station was in the far corner of the studio, next to a salon-style shampoo sink and a well-lit vanity table. The hairstylist and makeup artist were ready and waiting, the tools of their respective trades in place, as Tomás and Lilith walked up.

"Dino? Maureen? This is Lili Graves, Kristof's new discovery. I want you to make her ready for her close-up."

"That's what we're here for." Dino grinned, sticking a comb into the hip pocket of his bubblegum-pink designer jeans. "God! I can't *wait* to get my hands on your hair! Hop up in the chair, baby girl, so Mama and Daddy can get to work!"

Maureen leaned forward, closely scrutinizing Lilith's

face as if she were an art expert authenticating a masterpiece. "You have the most exquisite skin! It's like porcelain."

As Dino began parting Lilith's hair into two-inch sections, Maureen prepared the pressed powder for Lilith's T zone. "We're going for a subdued yet sophisticated look here," the makeup artist explained. "Something clean, with just a hint of radiance."

Lilith stared into the vanity mirror, awestruck by the sight of her own face. Her entire life she had been forced to steal glimpses of herself whenever she could, all the while fearful of being caught. Now she was free to look at herself as much as she wanted, and nobody seemed to think a thing about it. It felt incredibly natural yet at the same time oddly surreal, like flying while in a dream.

"I can't believe this is really happening," she muttered.

"Girlfriend, I *totally* know where you're coming from!" Dino chuckled. He had finished pinning her sectioned hair into mini-buns and was now misting them with a flexible-hold hair spray. "You are living the dream, hon! Living the dream!"

As Lilith stared at her mirror image, Kristof's face suddenly popped in over her shoulder. Although she was unable to turn her head, Lilith could see that there was a college-age brunette standing at the photographer's elbow, a clipboard folded under her arm. Lilith eyed the girl suspiciously. She didn't like the idea of other women hanging around Kristof.

"How is our star doing, Maureen?" Kristof asked.

"I've never worked on someone so relaxed before," Maureen said as she applied a shimmery nude pink shade to Lili's eyes. "Usually the new girls twitch or fidget, especially when I'm working on their eyes. Lili just sits there and lets me do my thing. It's wonderful!"

Lilith smiled, acknowledging Maureen's compliment. Sitting as still as a life-size doll while others toiled on her makeup and hair was as natural to her as breathing. After all, she'd been carefully groomed since earliest childhood by her personal dresser, a two-hundred-sixty-year-old undead gypsy girl named Esmeralda who had once been in charge of overseeing Madame de Pompadour's toilette.

"Lili, this is my assistant, Miriam," Kristof said, pointing to the girl with the clipboard. "She's handling all the paperwork for the shoot. She just needs you to fill out a few forms before we get started. Excuse me—I have to go talk to the lighting crew."

"Hi, Lili, I've got some ten-ninety-nines I need you to fill out," Miriam said, holding out the clipboard and a ballpoint pen.

"Ten-ninety-nines?" Lilith echoed, trying not to let on that she had no idea what they were.

"Uh-huh, it's for the IRS," Miriam explained. "I just need you to fill out your name, address, and Social

Security number in the proper boxes."

"Social Security number . . . ?" Lilith's guts began to cinch themselves into a knot. This was something she was completely unprepared for. She had imagined she would simply come to the studio, Kristof would take his pictures, and she would leave with a lot of money and fame. But now she was being asked to fill out forms and prove her identity—which was something of a problem, given that Lili Graves didn't actually exist.

"Uh-huh. You wouldn't happen to have your Social Security card on you, would you?"

"Sorry, I'm afraid I don't." The truth of the matter was that not only did she not have a Social Security card, Lilith didn't even know what Social Security actually *was*, save that the clots on TV were always yammering about it running out.

"Uh-huh. How about a driver's license I can Xerox?"

"I don't *have* a driver's license," Lilith replied, irritation starting to creep into her voice. "I don't drive."

"Who in Manhattan does, right?" Miriam said with a chuckle. "Okay, then—how about a student ID? Anything with your picture on it . . . ?"

By the Founders, the woman was *relentless*! Lilith took a deep breath as she tried to steady herself, her mind scrambling for an easy, believable lie that would extricate her from this situation.

"I'm afraid I left all my identification back at my

dorm at Columbia. I didn't realize I'd need it. I'm real new at all this. . . ."

"Uh-huh. That's all right, Lili. Just fill out as much as you can. I'll get what I need for our files at the next shoot."

"Next shoot?" Lilith asked as she quickly jotted down false information on the forms.

"Uh-huh. Maison d'Ombres has arranged for at least three different editorial shoots in *ELLE*, *Vogue*, and *Vanity Fair*," Miriam explained. "This is the *ELLE* shoot. Then there's the straight shoots for the advertising that's going to run in every major fashion and lifestyle periodical."

Kristof's assistant left, and Dino removed the pins from Lilith's hair, releasing a mass of loose waves. As he fastened her locks at the back of her head, he leaned down and whispered in Lilith's ear.

"How much are you getting for this shoot, sweetie?"

"I don't know," Lilith admitted. She had never thought twice about how she was being paid. Since Gala had gotten a million dollars, she had automatically assumed she would be getting a million dollars as well. "We really haven't talked about that aspect of it yet. . . ."

"That's what I was afraid of," the hairstylist said with a wry smile as he handed her a business card. "Here, take this. A friend of mine handles talent. Call him before this goes too far! You need a contract, girl, and you need one drawn up *fast*! I wouldn't trust *any-one* in this business, if I were you. They'll all smile in your face and tell you how beautiful and talented you are and then stab you in the back the first chance they get. Truth is they're all just a bunch of damned blood-suckers."

"Dino's right, hon," Maureen agreed as she carefully curled Lilith's lashes and applied a light coat of black mascara. "A girl as young and beautiful as you needs to have someone looking out for your best interests."

Lilith stared at the business card for a long moment before pocketing it. "You *really* think I'm beautiful?"

"Of *course* you are, sweetie!" Dino laughed. "Hasn't anyone told you that before?"

"All my life; I just didn't know whether they were lying or not."

"Silly girl! All you have to do is look in a mirror to know it's true."

"It's not as easy as that," Lilith replied wistfully. "Not for me, anyway."

Dino pursed his lips in dismay. "Models! I'll *never* understand how drop-dead gorgeous people can be so insecure!"

It was almost ten-thirty by the time Lilith was finished with hair and makeup. Then she was off to wardrobe. A tiny birdlike woman named Enid dressed her in her first ensemble for the day: a puffy buttercup-yellow dress with a black bow. Under normal circumstances Lilith wouldn't be caught wearing it dead in a Dumpster.

"Okay, Lili—here's what we're looking to do with this shoot," Tomás said as he walked her over to the waiting set. "We're playing up Maison d'Ombres being a French label. That's why our incredibly talented set designer and props master, Enrique, built this replica of a classic Parisian garret. You can even see the Eiffel Tower out your little window. Isn't that cute? Anyway, the theme of the editorial spread is that of a starving artist locked away in her loft, slave to her muse, just like Toulouse-Lautrec, except that you're young, hot, and have beautiful legs. You'll be portraying a poet, a painter, a sculptress, a dancer, a musician—each with a different Maison d'Ombres ensemble that allows you to express yourself. Do you think you can do that?"

"Mais oui." Lilith smiled.

Seven hours and five changes of clothes later, Kristof held up his hand and announced: "That's it, people! It's a wrap! We're done!"

Lilith, dressed in a red silk blouse cut to resemble a traditional painter's smock, put down the long-handled paintbrush she was pretending to use to finish an incomplete canvas depicting a man wearing a bowler hat with a green apple obscuring his face.

Maureen hurried forward from off camera and removed the daubs of color she had artfully smeared across the young model's cheek and brow to suggest paint.

"Let's hear it for our beautiful star: Lili Graves!" Tomás said as he stepped out from behind the LCD computer screen he was using to study the shots transferred from Kristof's digital camera. "I think I speak for everyone when I say that Lili really did a fantastic job here today!"

Lilith returned the borrowed clothes she was wearing to the stylist, heaving a sigh of relief as she changed back into the boot-cut jeans and cashmere sweater she had arrived in. As she zipped up her black leather Prada ankle boots, she glanced at her watch. It was after five in the afternoon, which meant it would be getting dark soon. If she hurried, she could get back to the penthouse in time to change into her school uniform before the night shift revived and discovered she was gone.

As she looked up from her watch, Lilith was surprised to find Kristof standing in front of her with an expectant look on his face. "I was wondering if you'd like to have dinner with me tonight."

"I'd *love* to, but it's getting late and I have, uh, night school this evening. I *really* need to leave. I'll get in trouble if I ditch class. . . ."

"I was hoping we could talk about your contract and the other shoots," Kristof said, looking somewhat crestfallen. "Plus, I have a present I wanted to give you. . . ."

"You got me a present?" Lilith asked excitedly. "What is it?"

"The only way you'll ever find out is if you agree to go to dinner with me." The photographer smiled.

Lilith glanced back at her watch. She really needed to leave if she was to get back to the penthouse before her absence was discovered, but she also wanted the present Kristof had promised her. And Lilith would gladly walk over a bed of live coals liberally garnished with rusty barbed wire and discarded syringes if there was a box with a bow waiting for her at the other end.

What to do? What to do . . . ?

"Did you really mean it when you told the others I did a fantastic job?" Lilith asked as the waiter placed her Niçoise salad in front of her.

"Of course I did! Like I said, I don't lie unless I'm in love. . . ."

"And even then, not until the third date," Lilith finished for him.

"And this is only our *second*." Kristof chuckled. "So you can still believe everything I say. And I'm telling you that you were truly incredible today, Lili."

Lilith smiled and lowered her eyes as she poked at her salad. She'd never spent so much time alone with a human before. Although, to be honest, she was finding it increasingly difficult to view Kristof as just another clot.

"So what's the present you wanted to give me?" Ever

since they'd left the studio, she'd been trying to guess what Kristof had bought for her. It had to be some little bauble or bangle, because all he was carrying on him was a leather portfolio about the size of a large notebook. Perhaps it was a tennis bracelet or a watch? Or a pair of earrings? It might even be a necklace or a ring.

"I have a present *and* a surprise for you. Which one do you want first?" he asked, giving her a mischievous smile.

"The present!"

"Here ya go, then." Kristof slid the leather portfolio across the tabletop.

The smile instantly disappeared from Lilith's face. Granted, the portfolio was made of fairly nice leather, but it wasn't like it was a purse or even a handbag. It didn't even have gold stamping on it or anything.

"Go ahead—look inside," he said.

Lilith flipped the portfolio open and saw a vaguely familiar young woman with piercing ice-blue eyes and honey-blond hair looking back at her. With a start, Lilith realized she was looking at pictures of her own face.

"These are the photos you took in your apartment!" she said as she paged through the plastic sleeves clipped within the portfolio's binder.

"Do you like them?"

"Kristof, no one's *ever* given me anything like this before in my life!" Lilith replied, and for once she was telling the absolute truth.

"Every real model has a portfolio—what she calls her 'book.' You take it with you on go-sees."

"Go-sees?" Lilith frowned.

"Job interviews with fashion designers and other potential clients," Kristof explained. He sighed and shook his head. "You really didn't think this whole thing out very well, did you?"

"What do you mean?" Lilith said defensively.

"Look, if we are going to continue to work together, you've got to be honest with me, especially about the important stuff, Lili."

"I don't understand what you're trying to say to me, Kristof."

"Lili, I *know* you're not eighteen. You listed your Social Security number as four-zero-three-two, for Christ's sake! You don't even know what a Social Security number is supposed to look like, do you?"

Lilith opened her mouth, prepared to launch into yet another round of denials, but then thought twice. It was better for her if Kristof mistook her for an underage girl pretending to be a college student rather than discover she was an underage vampire trying to pass herself off as human.

"You're right," she admitted, allowing her shoulders to slump.

"So how old are you *really*? Fifteen? Sixteen?"

"Sixteen."

Kristof took a deep breath and rubbed his face as if he'd suddenly become very tired. "Well, that's a good news/bad news situation. The good news is that being young isn't a drawback in this industry. Most models are your age."

"So what's the bad news?"

"There's not going to be a third date for us, I'm afraid. Not for several years, anyway. I have absolutely *no* interest in your father coming to look for me."

"I'm not scared of my dad," Lilith said sullenly.

"Well, that makes *one* of us." Kristof chuckled. "As it is, we're probably the same age."

"No, my dad's a *lot* older than you," she assured him. "And he's nowhere as cool. Fact is, he's a lying asshole. I need the money from this job so I can get out on my own and be free of my family. I'm *sick* of them trying to control my life and telling me what to do!"

"Well, that's not that unusual in this business, either." Kristof sighed. "Lili, I'm willing to go out on a limb here and help you lie about your age, your Social Security number, all of that. But I'll also see about hooking you up with a good lawyer who can help you emancipate yourself from your family, if that's what you really want. Do you want to know why I'm willing to take these risks? Because over fifty percent of the frames I shot of you today were usable."

"Is that good?"

"Kid, there are big-name supermodels I've worked

with who don't have that kind of percentage. With someone as green as you, it's unheard of. You're a phenom, Lili! If what you did today is any indication of the future, you're going to set the fashion world on fire. And I want to be there to watch it burn!"

"You said you had a surprise for me as well," Lilith said. "So what is it?"

"The publisher of *Vanitas* is throwing a Halloween party tonight. A lot of people from the industry will be there. I think it would be a great idea for you to meet these people and get some face time in with them. What do you say?"

Lilith glanced down at her watch. School was well under way by now. Although she knew she was already in trouble for playing hooky, she couldn't bring herself to worry about it. That was part of Lilith Todd's world, not Lili Graves's. Lili Graves was a girl without boundaries, limits, or expectations. And right now Lilith was enjoying her alter ego's life a lot more than her own.

"Sounds like fun," Lili replied.

CHAPTER ELEVEN

ally sighed as she walked through the cafeteria at Bathory Academy, looking for a table to sit at. Normally she took her midnight meal with Melinda and the Maledetto sisters, but she hadn't seen Melly since the incident on the pier, and her father had forbidden her to associate with the twins. It wouldn't be long before the other students realized she was flying solo once more, and then the hazing and harassment would begin again. With them, Cally feared, would come the risk of accidentally summoning the Shadow Hand.

The Vamps table was, of course, out of the question. Even though Lilith did not appear to be at school that evening, her second in command, Carmen, was jealously guarding their turf against all unworthy invaders.

Cally briefly contemplated sitting at the Amazon

table, but then thought better of it. Unless you were their equal in aerial combat and shapeshifting, the Amazons were more apt to give you a swirlie than pull out a chair in welcome. Cally was having to take Remedial Shapeshifting in an attempt to catch up with her peers, and she wasn't in that big a hurry to have them wash her hair.

That pretty much left the spod table, which was actually worse than sitting alone. The whole point was to avoid becoming a target, after all.

In the end she decided to run the risk of calling attention to herself and sat at an empty table. She frowned at her plastic bag of O poz. She hadn't really eaten much in the last couple of days, and although she knew she should be hungry, the best she could manage was a few sips.

"What in the name of the Founders do you think you're doing?"

Cally was surprised to see Melinda standing on the other side of the table, her hands planted on her hips and a scowl on her face.

"Melly! You're back!" Cally grinned, jumping to her feet to embrace her friend. "I was afraid the Van Helsings got you."

"Never mind about me," Melinda said, pushing Cally away. "I was sitting up with a sick friend. I want to know what's up with *you*, girl."

"What do you mean?"

Melinda stepped aside to reveal Bella and Bette standing behind her. On seeing the twins, Cally grabbed her tray and prepared to move to another table. Melinda sidestepped in front of her, blocking Cally's escape.

"I'm gone for one night and when I come back, it's to find you treating Bella and Bette like, well, like Lilith would! The only reason I'm not already kicking your ass is because I owe you. But that doesn't mean you can get away with acting like a complete and utter bitch on a stick."

"Are you mad at us, Cally?" Bette asked plaintively.

"No, I'm not mad at you, Bette." Cally sighed. "Neither you nor Bella has done anything wrong. This has nothing to do with you, really. It's my mom. She doesn't want me hanging out with you guys anymore."

"Why is your mother so worked up over the twins?" Melinda frowned.

Although she wanted to be honest with her friends, Cally doubted that telling them the whole truth would make things any easier. So she decided to tell them just a part of it instead. "Bella and Bette's brother gave me a ride home the other night, and my mom jumped to the wrong conclusion. Now she doesn't want me to have anything more to do with the Maledettos."

"You met our brother?" Bella asked in surprise.

"Didn't Lucky tell you?"

Bella shook her head. "We don't see Lucky that much anymore, now that he's working for Papa."

"Do you like him?" Bette asked.

"He seems nice." Cally shrugged.

"A lot of things aren't what they seem to be," Bella said, a grim look on her face. "Lucky is one of them."

Melinda snapped her fingers. "Can we get back to the subject at hand?" she asked tartly. "So what you're saying is that your mom doesn't want you hanging around the twins because she's got a thing against the Strega and is afraid you'll get mixed up with their big brother, is that it?"

"More or less," Cally said, relieved that she didn't have to lie any more than she had already.

Bella and Bette exchanged looks and then shared a deep sigh. "My sister and I understand the importance of family," Bette said solemnly as her sister nodded in agreement. "We respect your decision to honor your mother's wishes, even though it costs us your friendship."

Cally watched as the twins turned and walked away dejectedly, their heads down and shoulders slumped. Although she was relieved that Bella and Bette weren't mad at her, the sight of them looking so forlorn made Cally feel like she'd just hurled a bag full of fluffy little kitties into the river.

"I hope you're happy," Melinda said. "You get to dump your friends without having to feel guilty about it."

"I'm as far from happy as you could possibly imagine right now," Cally replied. "The last thing I wanted to do was treat them like Lilith does." She paused to look around the cafeteria. "Speaking of which, I haven't seen her around tonight."

"If I know her," Melinda said with a sour smile, "wherever she is right now, it's definitely rated triple X. You know: exciting, exclusive, and expensive."

The *Vanitas* Halloween party was being held in an event space in one of the old skyscrapers looking out onto Union Square. Waiters bearing silver trays laden with champagne and shrimp cocktails hurried in and out of the full-size kitchen, while costumed guests looked out the arched windows onto the park or lounged on the couches and ottomans scattered around the room.

Kristof led Lilith by the hand through the beautiful people, stopping every now and then to briefly chat with friends and business associates. After a few minutes of wandering through the crowd, the photographer succeeded in locating the hostess of the party: Fiona Alphew, publisher of *Vanitas*, one of the most respected publications in the fashion industry.

The millionaire publisher was dressed as Medusa, complete with realistic-looking viper hair extensions. She smiled warmly as Kristof approached her. "There you are!" she said. "I was afraid you weren't going to make it."

"You know I never miss your parties, my dear!" the photographer replied. "Besides, I wanted you to meet my newest discovery, Lili Graves."

"Oh. My. God!" Fiona gasped in admiration. "Wherever did you find her, Kristof? She is *stunning*!"

"It's a long story, darling—one that would make a sweet editorial piece," he said, winking as he gave her arm a gentle squeeze.

"Always the hustler!" The older woman laughed. "You better watch out, sweetie! He's a silver-tongued devil, this one."

Kristof snagged a couple glasses of champagne from a passing waiter, handing one to Lilith. She brought it up to her lips but did not actually drink. The moment Kristof turned back to continue chatting with Fiona, Lilith discreetly dumped her drink into a nearby potted plant.

"So who else is here?"

"Naomi is over there by the buffet—she's the one dressed like Marie Antoinette. And I saw Tyra hobnobbing with Anna just a few moments ago."

As Kristof turned to scan the crowded room, his face suddenly went pale. "Oh my God—what is *she* doing here? Shouldn't she still be in the hospital?"

Lilith followed the photographer's gaze and was surprised to see Gala sitting in a wheelchair on the other side of the room. Both of the model's legs were in plaster casts and strapped into what looked like combination cross-country ski boots and medieval torture devices. Standing behind her was a tall, sandy-haired man in his early thirties.

"It was the idea of that agent of hers," Fiona said sourly. "When he left Ford, he took her with him. She was his only real ticket."

"Well, I suppose I should go over and say hello," Kristof said, tossing back the rest of his drink. He took a deep breath and forced a smile onto his face before walking across the room. "Gala! Darling!"

"Kristof!" The model grabbed his hands and held on to them. Her smile was wide and desperate. "I was hoping you'd be here!"

"How are you feeling, dear? I must say I'm surprised to see you out so soon."

"You remember my agent, Derek, don't you?"

"Yes, of course," Kristof replied.

"I got a call from Karl yesterday," Derek blurted, his words slightly slurred from drink. "He expects Gala to give back her signing fee—or what's left of it, anyway. He's claiming she breached her contract."

"What? I'm sorry to hear that, Derek. I had no idea."

"It was an accident, Kristof! A bloody *accident*!" Derek's voice was loud enough to be heard over the surrounding cocktail party banter. "It's not Gala's fault she fell down the stairs and broke her legs!"

"I *was* drunk," Gala conceded, her eyes slightly glazed.

"Shut up!" Derek snapped. "Didn't I tell you to let *me* do the talking? You're on painkillers. You don't know what you're saying!"

"Look, Derek, I don't have any say over what Karl does," Kristof said, struggling to keep his voice calm. "He makes his decisions with Nazaire and that business partner of theirs. But you *had* to know we couldn't wait on Gala. Luckily, we managed to find a last-minute replacement." He turned and motioned for Lilith to join him. "Lili, come over here, will you? I'd like you to meet Gala."

As Lilith stepped forward, what little color remained in Gala's face drained away and her body began to shudder uncontrollably. Her head lolled back on her shoulders as foam spilled from her wildly champing jaws.

"She's having a seizure!" Derek shouted, looking about in alarm as his meal ticket began to spasm. "Somebody call nine-one-one!"

There was the sound of something liquid splashing against the hardwood floor, accompanied by the strong smell of ammonia. A shared cry of *"Eeewwww!"* arose from those nearest the wheelchair as they stepped back from the puddle spreading out across the floor.

"Gross!" Lilith grimaced, wrinkling her nose in disgust. "She peed herself!" She watched as the loser agent wheeled his former star out of the room like a broken toy, doing her best not to smile in triumph. It served the bitch right.

"She's worse off than I thought." Kristof shook his

head in disgust. "That girl needs to be in the hospital, not out networking."

As the waiter who drew the short straw arrived with a mop and bucket and began cleaning up the evidence of Gala's attendance at the party, Kristof took Lilith by the hand and led her away.

As she watched the costumed humans drink what seemed like an endless stream of wine and cocktails, Lilith found herself growing increasingly antsy. She was having about as much fun as a designated driver at the prom! She hated not being able to party with everyone else. Unlike the humans surrounding her, she could only get her drink on secondhand.

Suddenly her iPhone began to play Cobra Starship's "Smile for the Paparazzi." Lilith pulled it out of her purse and turned it off.

"Was that your boyfriend?"

"It was nothing that couldn't wait," she replied with a shrug.

"But you *do* have a boyfriend, don't you?" Kristof teased. "I mean, a beautiful young girl like yourself— I'd be really surprised if you didn't."

Lilith hesitated for a moment before finally nodding. She didn't want to give Kristof too much information about herself, but at the same time she was flattered by his interest, plus she found it hard to pass up an opportunity to talk about herself.

"You could call him that, I guess."

"Is it serious?"

"I used to think so—but now, I'm not so sure. Things have changed since we first got together."

"They always do at your age," Kristof said, giving her a reassuring pat on the shoulder. "Don't worry, it's only natural. Speaking of which, I need to take a quick trip to the gents before I reenact Gala's little show-stopper. I won't be long."

She hadn't been sober at a party since she was thirteen, and she wasn't about to go cold turkey now. It was just a question of figuring out who, when, and where—and pulling it off without drawing attention to herself. She cast her gaze about the room in search of suitable prey and quickly spotted a twentysomething dressed in a pirate costume who was having a little trouble staying on his feet. At first she thought he was simply in character, but as she watched him a little more closely, she realized he was not just drunk but positively stinko.

She walked up to the faux pirate, who was drinking a rum and Coke, and flashed him her patented smile.

"I like your costume."

"Thanks," the fake buccaneer said, trying hard to stand up straight. "My, um, my name is Tim, by the way."

"Hi, Tim. I'm Lili."

"Are you a model?"

"You could say that."

"That's cool," Tim the Pirate said, bobbing his head

up and down. "I'm, uh, I'm an intern."

"Aren't you kind of young to be a doctor?"

"Ha! Good one!" Tim laughed. "No, I work as an assistant over at *Vanitas*."

"That's cool, I guess," Lilith said. She had the clot on the hook. Now all she had to do was separate him from the herd as quickly as possible. "I'm going for some fresh air," she said, pointing at the door that opened onto the terrace. "Care to join me?"

"Don't mind if I do," Tim the Pirate Intern replied. "A little fresh air couldn't hurt right now."

It had taken Kristof longer than he'd thought to get in and out of the men's room. By the time he got back to the party, Lili was nowhere to be seen. He waved down a passing waiter who was carrying a tray of hors d'oeuvres.

"You didn't happen to see the young lady who was standing here a few minutes ago, did you?"

"You mean the smoking-hot blonde?" the waiter asked. "Last I saw, she went out on the terrace with some loser dressed like a pirate. I guess she was looking for a bit of the ol' Jolly Roger."

Suddenly the French doors swung open and Lili reentered the room, sans her buccaneer beau. Kristof looked out onto the terrace and saw the young man slumped across a marble bench next to the railing.

"What happened to your friend?" Kristof asked.

Lilith didn't know what Tim the Pirate had been guzzling, popping, snorting, and smoking earlier that night, but she was riding a pretty good buzz.

She giggled. "I'm afraid he's walked the plank."

Cally looked out the window of the train as it sped along the Williamsburg Bridge toward the lights of Brooklyn. She flipped her cell phone open and paged through the address book until she found the number she was looking for. Taking a deep breath, she closed her eyes and punched the call button. As she counted the rings on the other end, she told herself she had to be out of her mind for doing this.

"Hello?"

Cally was so startled by the sound of Jules's voice in her ear she nearly dropped the phone. "Oh! Hi! I thought it was going to go to voice mail," she said with a nervous laugh.

"Who is this?" Jules asked. Cally could hear the muted, jackhammer thump of high-volume dance beats in the background. "Lilith? Is that you?"

"No. It's Cally. You gave me your number a couple of nights ago, remember?"

"Oh! Hi, Cally!" Jules's voice brightened. "Give me a second, okay—I'm going to go where it's easier to talk." There was the sound of movement on the other end, followed by the creak of a door opening. Suddenly the background noise dropped substantially. "There. That's better." Jules sighed in relief. "So—did you change your mind about the Grand Ball?"

"Well, I'm, uh, calling, aren't I?"

"Cool! You want me to be your escort?"

"Yes. Assuming you're still available, that is?"

"Of course I still want to be your escort. But I thought you said you didn't want to antagonize Lilith. Aren't you afraid of making her mad?"

As Cally pondered Jules's question, she suddenly became aware of an odd sensation in her left hand as it rested atop her knee. It kind of felt like the tingling sensation she'd experienced when her stormgathering ability had first started to manifest itself when she was thirteen. The difference was that the feeling associated with stormgathering came from without, while this seemed to be coming from within, as if some unseen force was gathering itself inside her hand.

"Not anymore," Cally replied.

CHAPTER TWELVE

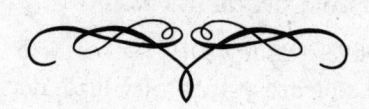

It was just after sunrise when Lilith returned home. Since her parents normally retired to their separate bedchambers just before the break of dawn, Lilith had hoped she would be able to sneak back into their penthouse apartment unnoticed.

Instead, the elevator doors opened to reveal a seething Victor Todd pacing the private lobby like a caged animal.

"Where have you been, young lady?" Victor growled, snatching his daughter by the arm and yanking her out of the elevator.

"Let go of me!" Lilith yelped as her father dragged her into the apartment.

"You weren't in your bedroom when the servants came to wake you this evening, and I know it wasn't because you were in a hurry to get to school. Madame

Nerezza called to *personally* inform me that you never arrived at the academy!" Victor snarled angrily as he slammed the door behind them.

"You're squeezing my arm!"

"I should squeeze your pretty little neck! You really had us worried, Lilith! For all your mother and I knew, you were lying in a ditch somewhere with a stake through your heart."

"A lot you care!" Lilith retorted, pulling herself free of her father's grasp. "The only reason you'd hate to see me dead is because that would mean you'd have to start sleeping in the same bed as my mother again."

"How *dare* you speak to me like that?" Victor gasped. "Are you drunk?"

"Well, *duh*," Lilith sneered. "I *always* come home drunk, Daddy! You'd know that if you actually paid any attention."

"Where'd you get that?" Victor asked, pointing to the leather portfolio she was holding.

"It's nothing; it's just a notebook, that's all," Lilith replied, hiding it behind her back.

"If it's nothing, then you shouldn't have any problem letting me look at it," Victor said as he tried to snatch the portfolio out of his daughter's hands.

"Leave me alone!" Lilith shouted. "It's *mine*! You can't have it!"

"I've had enough of this foolishness, Lilith!" Victor said angrily. "You're grounded until further notice."

Lilith's jaw dropped as if the muscles had been severed. "I'm *what*?!"

"You heard me. Your grades at school are horrible. From here on in there will be no more partying with those friends of yours until the break of dawn instead of studying. I'm also canceling all your platinum cards— you'll have to make do with a single gold card."

"You can't do this to me!" Lilith pouted, stamping her foot in protest. "You're being totally unfair."

"No, 'totally unfair' would be if I decided to keep you home from the Grand Ball," her father retorted.

"You wouldn't dare!" she said, tears forming in her eyes. "I'm to be the final presentation of the night!"

"Oh, but I *would*. And I *shall*. That is, unless you tell me where you have been tonight and who you were with."

Lilith was in the tightest spot of her life. She had used every tactic that normally resulted in her father capitulating to her will: shouting, whining, pouting, and crying. There was only one move left for her to play. She instantly ceased her crocodile tears and fixed Victor with a look of unalloyed hatred.

"Very well, if that's how it's going to be, you leave me no choice. I'm going to tell Irina *all* about your precious little Cally."

"*What?*" Now it was Victor's turn to look stunned.

"That's right, Daddy!" Lilith smirked. "I know about your secret daughter. And if you don't start being very,

very nice to me, Mother will know, too! You wouldn't want *that* to happen, would you, Father dear? So, if you know what's good for you—and your bastard daughter—you'll keep your hands off my platinum cards. Have I made myself understood?"

"All too well," Victor replied stonily.

Cally was buttoning the white blouse of her school uniform when she heard the doorbell ring.

"Mom! Somebody's at the door!"

The doorbell rang a second time, followed by a loud knock.

"Mom—the door!" Cally shouted again.

When it became obvious that her mother was not going to respond, Cally stomped out of her room, muttering under her breath. She glanced at her mother's bedroom, the door to which was still shut. No doubt Sheila was nursing yet another hangover.

Cally peered through the peephole into the hall and saw two tall, moderately well-built men, one blond, the other with brown hair, both dressed in matching dark collarless suit jackets and turtleneck sweaters. They also wore wraparound sunglasses. She opened the door a crack and looked around the doorjamb. "Yes? May I help you?"

Without warning, the blond man pushed against the door with surprising strength, and he and his companion bulldozed their way into the foyer.

"What do you two think you're doing?" Cally yelled.

"You can't barge in here like that!"

The blond man silently pointed to the back of the apartment. The dark-haired man nodded and headed down the hallway in the direction of the bedrooms, while the blond walked into the living room.

"Hey! Where do you think you're going?" Cally shouted, hurrying after the dark-haired intruder. "Get out before I have to hurt you and your friend!"

"It's all right, Cally. They mean you no harm. They're with me."

Cally turned to find Victor Todd standing at the front door.

"Dad?" Cally frowned. "What are you doing here? What's going on? Who are these creeps?"

"Their names are Walther and Sinclair. They are servants of mine," Victor explained, closing the door behind him. "You must forgive their rather brusque manner, but they've only recently been reawakened. I've had them in cold storage since 1965. I cannot rely on undead created in the last century, as they are equally under my wife's control. Sinclair has spent three hundred years in service to the Todds and Walther even longer."

Cally stared at the blond man, who was busy taking every book off the shelves in the living room and placing them into tidy stacks on the floor. "They're undead?"

"Yes. But you have nothing to fear from them," her

father assured her. "Walther and Sinclair recognize you as family, and they are under strict orders not to feed on your mother."

"Well, that's something of a relief, I guess." She pointed at the blond undead, who was still stacking books. "Which one is he?"

"That's Walther."

"Thanks." Cally put her fingers in her mouth, whistled, and shouted: "Hey, Walther!"

The blond undead stopped and turned to face her. "Yes, young mistress?"

"What are you doing?"

"I am preparing your belongings for packing."

"What?"

Cally turned and ran down the hallway and into her room. As she slid to a stop in the open doorway, she saw that Sinclair was diligently removing each article of clothing from the wardrobe and neatly folding it before placing it atop her bed.

"Get out of my room!" Cally shouted. "Who said you could come in here and start touching my stuff?!"

The door to her mother's bedroom opened to reveal Sheila Monture, sans makeup and dressed in a ragged housecoat. *"What the hell is going on? I'm trying to get some rest!"* Sheila froze when she saw her former lover standing in the hallway. "Victor? What are you doing here?"

"Don't touch that!" Cally snatched one of her dresses

from Sinclair and returned it to the wardrobe.

Sinclair reached in and pulled the same dress back out.

"I said don't touch it!" Cally repeated angrily, yanking the garment out of the undead servant's hands again and shoving it once more into the wardrobe.

Sinclair, his face registering no signs of irritation or surprise, removed the dress for a third time.

"What is this guy's malfunction?" Cally groaned in exasperation.

"There's no point in trying to stop him, Cally," Victor explained. "You'll give up long before he will. The undead never grow weary. Once they're given a task, they will complete it no matter how long it takes or how arduous it might be."

"Why are they here? And what's this about packing our things?" Cally asked, turning to face her father.

"You and your mother are leaving New York."

"What do you mean we're leaving?" Sheila frowned.

"Cally is in grave danger. You must leave the city as soon as possible. I have one-way tickets to Sweden already booked—"

"Sweden?!" Cally yelped. "You've got to be kidding me."

"I realize it's far away, but you should be safe there."

"Safe from what?" Sheila asked nervously.

Victor turned to face her, his manner grim. "Lilith

knows that Cally is my daughter."

"What?" Sheila gasped. "Are you sure?"

Victor nodded. "She threatened to go to her mother with the information when I said I was going to ground her for playing hooky from school."

"How could she have possibly found out?" Sheila said.

Victor turned to Cally, fixing her with a stern gaze. "Has Lilith tasted your blood?"

Cally nodded. "We got into a fight at school," she said sheepishly. "She bit me on the shoulder."

"Well, there's no point crying over shed blood," Victor said. "What's done is done. It's only a matter of time before Lilith tells her mother the truth. The only reason she hasn't done so yet is because she and her mother are not close."

"Where in Sweden are you sending us?" Cally asked.

"There is a hunting lodge that belonged to my father, located twelve kilometers out of Kiruna, the northern-most city in the country. It's actually in Lapland, near the Arctic Circle. I have arranged for servants loyal to the Todd bloodline to tend to you there. I will also arrange for tutors so that you are properly educated while you're in seclusion."

"How long will we have to stay there?" Cally asked.

"Ten, maybe twenty years. By that time, you should have sufficient expertise to protect yourself against Irina, given that you learn to master the Shadow Hand."

"Ten years?" Cally wailed, a stricken look on her face. "But I *like* it in New York! This is so not fair. Just when I'm finally making friends at school and I get invited to the Grand Ball, I have to move to the North Pole!" She plopped down on the edge of her bed, tears welling in her eyes. "This is bullshit. I don't *want* to move to Sweden. You can't *make* me!"

"I'm not doing this to be mean, Cally," Victor said gently. "I'm trying to save your life—and your mother's."

"Can't you at least let me attend the Grand Ball before sending me away?" Cally pleaded. "Rauhnacht is this weekend. I'll do as you ask if you'll just let me go."

"It won't work. There's no way I can publicly acknowledge you as my daughter. And the rules forbid girls from being presented unless they have a father or other male relative to introduce them."

"I realize that, but I just thought maybe you could get someone to at least *pretend* to be my dad."

Victor paused, a thoughtful look crossing his face. "You know, having someone else say you're his daughter might make Lilith's claims less believable." He nodded. "Very well, I will arrange a surrogate for you. But you have to promise me you won't tell *anyone* you're leaving the country, understand?"

"Thank you!" Cally exclaimed, throwing her arms around Victor's neck. "Thank you! Thank you! *Thank you!* You're the best father in the world!"

"Well, I'm glad at least *one* of my daughters thinks so." Victor chuckled. "Go ahead and attend school tonight. But try to steer clear of Lilith as much as possible."

"So she knew I was her sister all this time," Cally said sourly, shaking her head. "And she *still* treated me like crap. And to think, I actually felt guilty for not liking her when I learned the truth. What a bitch." She grimaced and gave her father an apologetic look. "Sorry about that."

"Don't be," Victor said.

The car phone was ringing as Victor Todd climbed into his Rolls Tungsten. He tapped the communications panel of the LCD display built into the back of the front passenger seat, activating the car's hands-free system.

"Talk to me," he said by way of greeting.

"Victor? It's Karl." The disembodied voice that came through the Rolls's sound system was that of Victor's most trusted vassal, Baron Karl Metzger, who handled several of the Todd family's investments.

"How's the weather in Paris?"

"Much like New York, this close to Rauhnacht," Metzger replied. "I was calling to see if you received the package I sent?"

Victor glanced over at the unopened padded envelope

sitting on the seat next to him. It had been delivered to the penthouse just as he was leaving to retrieve Walther and Sinclair from the cold-storage warehouse. "I have it with me, but I haven't had a chance to look at it yet."

Although HemoGlobe was Victor's primary business and moneymaker, he had long ago learned the wisdom of diversifying into other fields of endeavor. After all, a wise man doesn't keep all his blood in one cellar. Over the decades he had sunk funds into numerous businesses, ranging in everything from farm implements to telecommunications.

"I just need you to look at them and give me your okay before I sign off on the new contract for the replacement. My son and I will take everything from there."

"Very well." Victor sighed. "I'll take a look." He picked up the envelope and opened it, pulling out the proof sheet.

He made a strangled, snarling noise as he saw the blond hair and ice-blue eyes of the model, and the photographs slid from his numbed hands and across the floor of the luxury sedan.

"Is something wrong, my liege?"

Victor Todd did not answer but instead wrenched the LCD panel from its mounting and hurled it out the closed window of the speeding car and into the streets of Brooklyn in a spray of shattered safety glass.

* * *

Although virtually all his paying work was done with a digital SLR camera, Kristof still preferred to shoot at least one or two rolls of 35-mm film with his old Leica. While digital cameras were far more cost-effective and granted instantaneous knowledge of what shots were worth keeping, traditional film allowed him latitude in high-contrast situations, revealing a world of detail in the highlights and shadows that could never be coaxed from a digital file.

It was because of this appreciation for the inherent poetry of black-and-white photography and old-school optical lab techniques that Kristof had turned his second bathroom into a darkroom.

In the blood-red glow of the light, he watched as Lili's face gradually appeared on the exposed print paper floating in the developer tray, like a ghost emerging from a fog bank.

As Kristof quickly transferred the print from the developer tray to the stop bath with a pair of tongs, then moved it to the fixer tray, he thought he heard someone moving around in his combination sleeping area/office/living room.

It was probably his assistant, Miriam. She was always forgetting something. Last time it was her purse. The time before that it was her laptop. Setting the timer for two minutes, he opened the door to the darkroom and stuck out his head.

"Miriam—is that you?"

He waited for a reply, but all he heard was silence. He shrugged and ducked back inside the darkroom as the timer went off. It must have been the building settling or the upstairs neighbors coming home.

He removed the black-and-white print from the fixer tray and placed it in the wash, swishing it back and forth with his tongs. As he looked down at the print floating in the distilled water, Kristof noticed for the first time what appeared to be a double exposure.

As he pulled the photograph out of the rinse tray and clipped it to the drying line strung across the bathtub, he could clearly see the outline of the Eiffel Tower superimposed over Lili's face. But that was impossible. He'd triple-checked all his cameras before the shoot for light leaks and film misfeeds.

Kristof's frown deepened even further when he discovered that the double exposure did not seem to affect either the clothing the model was wearing or the surrounding props and scenery. Although her features were still visible, it was as if she had suddenly been transformed into glass. How the hell was it possible for Lili to be the only thing affected in the entire frame?

Looking more closely, Kristof realized that the Eiffel Tower on Lili's face was not the haphazard result of one exposure being taken atop another, but the simple fact he was looking *through* Lili's head at what she was standing in front of, which just happened to be the fake window with its pretend view of the Eiffel Tower.

"What the—?" he muttered, snatching the print off the line.

Kristof turned around to discover he was no longer alone. Standing between him and the darkroom door was a tall man with dark hair gone gray at the temples, his eyes glowing like those of an animal.

"What do you think you're doing with my daughter?" the intruder growled, flashing fangs as white and sharp as those of a wolf.

Kristof didn't have time to explain, but he did manage to scream.

CHAPTER THIRTEEN

T wo in the morning is the time when most reasonable people have long gone to bed and the unreasonable start to consider heading home. For the students of Bathory Academy, however, it means school is out and the rest of the night is their own.

For Lilith Todd, that normally meant spending the few hours before dawn partying with her entourage in the VIP room at the Belfry. As she exited the blood-red doors of Bathory Academy, Lilith spotted Bruno, her chauffeur, standing by the rear passenger door of the Rolls, stoically awaiting her arrival as he did every school night.

"To the club, Bruno," she said with a toss of her head. Her smile disappeared on seeing her father in the backseat of the sedan.

"Daddy! What a surprise! I wasn't expecting you."

"I know," Victor growled. "You're not going to the club tonight—or any other night."

"Haven't you forgotten our little agreement?" Lilith said testily. "You don't tell me what I can and can't do, and I don't tell dear mother about your little . . . indiscretion."

"It would seem I am not the only one in this family guilty of being indiscreet," Victor snarled, holding up the leather portfolio Kristof had given Lilith the night before. "Now get in the car!"

"Where did you get that?!" she gasped.

"From your bedroom."

"How dare you go in my room without my permission?"

"*Your* room?" Victor said with a humorless laugh. "All that you have in the world is that which *I* have chosen to give you. Now get in the damn car!"

"Give it back!" Lilith cried as she tried to make a grab for the portfolio. "That's mine. Kristof gave it to me."

"How could this possibly belong to you?" Victor taunted, holding the portfolio just beyond his daughter's grasp. "Kristof gave this to Lili Graves, not Lilith Todd."

Lilith froze, a startled look on her face. "How did you know about that?"

"I know a great deal about 'Lili'—or at least *now* I do," Victor said. "After all, I *do* own Maison d'Ombres."

Lilith gasped in disbelief. "*You're* Nazaire d'Ombres?"

"No, Maison d'Ombres is one of my more recent acquisitions. Considering how much you and your mother spend on couture, I decided it might make for a profitable side venture."

Lilith looked around nervously as the limo pulled away from the curb. "Where are we going? Back home?"

"No," her father replied. "I thought we should visit a mutual business acquaintance first."

They were two blocks from Kristof's loft when Lilith saw the police barricades blocking the middle of the street. A weary cop was standing on the curb, alternately sipping coffee from a ubiquitous blue-and-white paper cup and talking into his two-way radio.

As Victor powered down the rear window, the acrid stink of heavy smoke wafted into the limo. "Excuse me, Officer," he said politely. "But what seems to be the holdup?"

"There was a fire in an apartment building up the street here," the policeman replied, pointing in the direction of Kristof's. "It was burning pretty good for a while, but it looks like they finally got it under control. We have to keep the block sealed off because of the fire trucks."

"Oh, dear," Victor said. "I do hope no one was hurt."

"The EMTs hauled off some guy who lived there for

smoke inhalation. Photographer or something. The fire started in his darkroom."

"Thank you, Officer," Victor said as he closed the window. He turned to look at his daughter, who was glaring at him with undisguised hatred.

"Don't you *dare* hurt Kristof!" she said, her voice trembling in both fear and anger.

"My dear, if I wanted to kill him, he would already be dead. You needn't concern yourself over the photographer's well-being, if for no other reason than that he's needed for the Maison d'Ombres launch campaign.

"I assure you, he is unharmed. However, I did take the liberty of erasing *all* memory of you—or should I say Lili Graves—from his mind. I'll leave it to Metzger and his son to mind-wipe the others who may have come in contact with you. As for the fire, it was never meant to kill Kristof, just destroy all physical evidence of Lili Graves's existence.

"I have no idea what you were trying to prove with this idiotic stunt of yours, but praise to the Founders I was able to nip it in the bud before it was too late! Lilith, do you have any concept of what you risked doing this?" Victor asked, shaking his head in bewilderment. "Do you realize how close you came to being dragged away by the Crimson Guard and publicly executed as a traitor to the Blood? The moment someone recognized your face in a magazine or on a billboard and reported it to the Synod, the Lord Chamberlain would have signed your death warrant without any hesitation. I cannot believe a child of my issue could do something so incredibly stupid!"

"But you didn't have to do it like this!" Lilith sobbed. "You could at least let me keep Kristof!"

"No, I couldn't," Victor said grimly as he reached inside the portfolio. He pulled out a black-and-white print and showed it to his daughter.

Lilith's face blanched and her hands began to tremble even more than before as she stared at the Eiffel Tower outlined against her face as if etched in crystal.

"By becoming involved with Kristof, you not only risked calling attention to the existence of vampires, but you jeopardized your marriage to Jules as well. If Count de Laval ever finds out about these pictures, he will negate the contract between the families."

"But I didn't have sex with Kristof," Lilith protested.

"*That's* not the point!" Victor snapped. "As a member of the aristocracy, you're expected to show both wisdom and tact. What you've done is not only recklessly selfish, but self-destructive as well. Those are qualities that can spell disaster to even the most powerful house. By the Outer Dark, what patriarch in his right mind would allow his heir apparent to become bound to a bride capable of such childish idiocy?

"While you may not be my only daughter, you are the one who bears my name. Since I have no sons to continue the House of Todd, I've worked hard to ensure that our family's genetic legacy and bloodright isn't usurped by weaving it into the tapestry of one of the most influential and powerful aristocratic families in the world.

"I want to get three things straight between us. First, you will cease making attempts on your sister's life. . . ."

"Did *she* tell you I tried to kill her?" Lilith snarled. "What a sniveling little snitch. And she's *not* my sister!"

"Very well, then you will cease making attempts on your *demi-sister's* life. Second, if you so much as *whisper* Cally's name around your mother, I swear by Tanoch the Stormgatherer, I will take these photographs and turn them over to the Synod myself! And last, but most importantly, if you *ever* try to blackmail me again, whether you're my heiress or not, I *shall* destroy you."

"You wouldn't *dare*!" Lilith replied, trying to hide the quaver of uncertainty in her voice.

"Wouldn't I?" Victor said coldly. "I didn't get where I am today without being willing to shed the blood of my kin. And as you know, I *do* have another daughter. . . ."

Cally sat and stared at the dressmaker's dummy Granny had given her for her thirteenth birthday. Save for a couple of minor embellishments here and there, Cally was pretty much finished with her evening gown for the Grand Ball. And in her opinion, it was every inch as kick-ass as the designer gowns Melinda and the twins had paid thousands of dollars for. Take *that*, House of Dior!

If someone had told Cally a month ago that she would be a debutante at the Rauhnacht Grand Ball, she would have laughed. But here she was, less than forty-eight hours away from making her social "debut" to New York City's Old Blood elite. And as usual, she found herself with conflicted emotions.

While she was excited by the pageantry and ritual of it all, another part of her was distressed by the fact that she was participating under false pretenses. Not only was she claiming to be the daughter of a man who was not her father, but she wasn't even a true-born vampire. Then again, what did it matter? She was leaving for Sweden the moment the ball was over.

It was hard to believe that within seventy-two hours she would be on a snowmobile, headed into the Arctic Circle. After a lifetime spent in the hustle and bustle of New York City, she might as well be going to the moon. The idea of not looking out her window and being able to see the bridge and the lights of the city was almost too much to bear. And who would tend her grandparents' grave once she was gone? She hated to think of Granny's headstone becoming as weathered and unkempt as those residents of Rest

Haven who no longer had visitors.

Not being able to tell any of her friends good-bye was tough, but she could do it. What was hard was leaving the one person she truly cared about.

Breaking up with Peter had been the hardest thing she'd ever done, but she did it to protect him. Still, it saddened her to think that they might never be together again. She didn't want him to go through life thinking she no longer cared. The possibility of never seeing his face or hearing his voice was enough to crack her heart like an egg.

Cally got up and tiptoed into the living room to make sure her mother was asleep. Sure enough, Sheila was sprawled on the chaise lounge, snoring softly, her wireless headphones still clamped around her ears. The undead servants her father had left behind were busy in the darkened kitchen, stoically wrapping dishware in newspaper and packing it into cardboard boxes. Satisfied the coast was as clear as it was likely to get, Cally returned to her bedroom and locked the door behind her before calling Peter's number on her cell phone.

After several rings, a groggy-sounding voice finally answered.

"Hello?"

"I'm sorry I'm calling so late, Peter."

"Cally? Is that you?" Peter was suddenly wide

awake. "I miss you so much."

"I'm sorry I said what I did," she apologized. "I didn't really mean it. I said a *lot* of things that night I didn't mean."

"Me too, Cally," Peter said. "It's just that I was so afraid of losing you. Sometimes I start talking before I start thinking, if you know what I mean?"

"Yeah, I do," she said, smiling into the receiver. "I'm so sorry things went so wrong between us. I don't want you to think I hate you. What I feel for you is anything *but* hate. It's just that I'm so afraid. . . ."

"Afraid of what?"

"Of you getting hurt, that's all. It would tear me apart if anything happened to you because of me."

"Cally, I feel the same way you do," Peter said passionately. "Every time one of the others tells me they've staked a sucker—I mean, killed a vampire—my heart stops, and I pray it's not you they're talking about. If only we could run away and put all of this behind us and start fresh somewhere. . . ."

"Believe me, there's nothing I would love more than that." She sighed sadly. "But I'm afraid it's just not possible. At least, not now, anyway."

"What do you mean?"

Cally took a deep breath, then said, "Peter, the real reason I'm calling you is . . . I just wanted you to know how I feel before—"

"Before what?" he asked, an edge of suspicion in his voice.

"I leave New York."

"You're leaving the city? Why?"

"My father is sending me and my mother to Europe to try and protect us from his wife."

"Europe?!" Peter groaned as if he'd just been hit in the gut. "When are you coming back?"

"I don't know. Maybe not for a very long time."

"I don't want you to go away, Cally!" Peter protested. "You belong here with me!"

"I don't want to go, Peter, but there's nothing I can do."

Peter paused for a moment as what she had said began to sink in.

"How much time do we have before you go?"

"I'm leaving immediately after the Grand Ball on Rauhnacht."

"Rauhnacht? But that's this weekend, isn't it? There must be *something* you can do that will make Todd reconsider!"

Cally took the cell phone from her ear and stared at it for a long moment, as if she could see through the earpiece to the other side. "Peter," she said icily, "how do you know that Victor Todd is my father?"

"I—I—didn't say that," he stammered.

"Yes. You. *Did*. I just *heard* you."

"Oh. Uh. You must have mentioned it to me earlier

and just forgot," Peter said quickly. Suddenly he sounded very nervous.

"No, I *didn't*, Peter. I was afraid you might hate me if you knew I was the daughter of your father's arch-enemy, so I made sure I didn't mention his name."

"Oh. Well. Uh."

As she listened to Peter hem and haw, trying to figure a way out of his lie, the truth, as cold as morning at the South Pole, dawned on Cally.

"You knew who my father was all along, didn't you?" she said in wounded disbelief. "And you never said a word even though you *knew* it was important to me! Why? *Why* would you do such a thing to me, Peter? Were you just pretending to be my friend and care about me so I would lower my guard?"

"No, Cally—that's not it at all!" Peter said frantically. "I was afraid *you'd* turn against *me* if you knew you were Todd's daughter! I was just trying to protect what we had between us!"

"You know what, Peter? Before I called you, I was really upset that I had to go away, but now I'm really, *really* glad I'm leaving."

"Cally, no! Don't hang up!" Peter begged. "I *love* you, Cally! Living without you is torture!"

"Good! Suffer, then!" Cally said angrily, snapping the cell phone shut.

As she wiped the tears from her eyes, she told herself it was all for the best. Things never could have worked out for them. Besides, Peter was all wrong for her, and she'd never really loved him in the first place.

It was all another lie, of course. But if she kept telling it to herself over and over, maybe she'd come to believe it was true.

CHAPTER FOURTEEN

Lilith peered out the window of the Rolls at Saint Germain's Fine Books, a few blocks east of Grand Central Terminal. A sign on the door announced: BY APPOINTMENT ONLY.

"What are we doing here?" she asked. "I thought we were going home."

"*We* are not doing anything here," her father said. "*You* are coming here to study after school."

"But Jules and the others are waiting for me at the Belfry!"

"And they will *continue* to wait until your grades have improved!" Victor retorted. "Until then, Bruno is under orders to drive you to only three destinations: home, school, and here, the Central Scrivenery. I advise you to enjoy the Grand Ball as much as possible, because that is going to be the *last* chance you have to

see your friends outside of school for a very long time."
Victor leaned across his daughter and opened the door.
"Bruno will be back to pick you up before dawn."

Lilith found herself in a huge, circular room the size of an
Olympic skating rink. The ceiling loomed stories above
her head. At first glance it resembled a cross between a
cave, a beehive, and a public library. The walls of the
scrivenery were sixty feet high and lined with numerous hand-carved niches, like those found in catacombs.
Inside each niche were stacks of leather scroll cases. Lilith
could see winged figures flitting back and forth from
niche to niche, alternately pulling and returning scroll
cases for those down below.

The floor of the scrivenery itself was crowded with
reading tables and copying desks arranged in a dimin-
ishing spiral, resembling the ringed chambers of a
nautilus. At the center of the great chamber stood the
Master Scrivener's desk, which towered over the lesser
tables like a judge's bench.

"Please make yourself comfortable," one of the assistant scriveners said, gesturing to the desks. "What scroll
do you seek?"

"I dunno," Lilith said, shrugging her shoulders. "I'm
flunking my alchemy class."

"Alchemy, eh? Wait right here. I will be back shortly."
The scrivener shed his human guise and, with a single
flap of leathery wings, took to the air, flying up to a

niche thirty feet above the chamber's floor.

He returned a moment later and handed a two-foot-long leather document tube to Lilith.

"Here you go," he said. "Should you require any other documents, just raise your hand and one of our staff will be happy to assist you."

"Yeah. Whatever." She shrugged. "Thanks, I guess."

Lilith waited until the spoddy apprentice dude, or whatever he was supposed to be, had walked away before unfastening the lid on the document tube and sliding its contents onto the table.

This was so incredibly stupid. It was bad enough her father had derailed her career as a supermodel, but now he was actually forcing her to study. Yuck. If Victor thought he'd frightened her into abandoning her dreams of striking out and becoming her own woman, he was seriously deluded. Oh, sure, she'd played all cowed and tearful and promised that she had learned her lesson, but in reality all dear Daddy succeeded in doing was hardening her resolve.

She had gone into modeling completely blind. Still, despite her ignorance of how things were done in the world of humans, she had succeeded in going pretty far, very fast. Now that she knew how easy it was to be someone else, she had a taste for the excitement and novelty that came with living a double life. With a well-placed bribe or two, she was sure she could acquire a Social Security card and other forms of ID she'd need to move freely among humans.

Still, her father's threats aside, there was the unavoidable fact that her image was already starting to fade away, at least on traditional film stock. That meant it was only a matter of time before she would be invisible to digital cameras.

It seemed ludicrous to her that humans, who lived lives as short as mice compared to her people, could have figured out how to transplant organs, fly to the moon, and split the atom. Yet no one, in the twenty thousand years the vampire race had walked this world, had tried to address this serious drawback to their people. Perhaps it was time to take a page from the humans. After all, they spent billions on creams and lotions in an attempt to postpone, if not reverse, the effect of aging. If they could do it—why couldn't she?

Her father had triggered a cultural revolution the likes of which had never been seen before, simply by making the hunting of humans no longer necessary for the survival of vampires. But imagine the changes that would result if her people no longer had to fear reflective surfaces and cameras. The resulting shock waves would make Victor Todd's contribution to vampire society look like the hula hoop or Pac-Man.

Lilith smiled at the thought of her father being reduced to a footnote. She liked that idea. Yeah, she liked it a lot.

Surely, among all the centuries of collected information stored in the Central Scrivenery, there was something that might answer this question. But how to find it? How could she hope to figure out an answer to the most serious impediment to the vampire race's continued survival: the lack of a reflection? She was flunking out of Basic Alchemy, for crying out loud.

"What are *you* doing here?"

Lilith looked up to find Xander Orlock standing on the other side of the reading table, a parchment case in one hand and a scrivening kit in the other. He was still dressed in his Ruthven's school uniform, the tie loosened and pulled slightly askew. He was so pale the blue veins in his hands and face were visible through his skin, and his long fingers reminded Lilith of spider legs. His champagne-colored hair was brushed back from his high, wide forehead and worn in a pronounced widow's peak. With his pointed ears, arched eyebrows, and unretractable fangs, there was no way he could pass as human, but as Orlocks go, he wasn't too hideous. Still, he *was* an Orlock.

"What's it look like I'm doing?" she replied, not bothering to hide her irritation.

"Are you sure you haven't made a wrong turn somewhere? This isn't a nightclub."

"Duh! I hadn't noticed," Lilith said, rolling her eyes for emphasis. "If you *must* know, I'm here to study for my stupid alchemy class. If I don't pass, I'm going to flunk out of Bathory."

"Bummer." He cleared his throat and pointed to the chair opposite from Lilith. "Do you mind if I sit with you?"

"You're kidding, right?" she said, fixing him with an icy stare.

The hopeful look on Xander's face quickly disappeared and his shoulders dropped.

As he turned to leave, it suddenly occurred to Lilith that the answer to her problem was about to slip between her fingers. If anyone could invent her new cream it was Exo. She quickly pasted on her most winning smile and hurried after her target.

"Exo, I mean, Xander—come back!" she said, touching him on the arm. "Don't be silly! Of course you can sit here with me! I was just joking with you."

"Really?" he said, dazzled by the smile Lilith flashed him. "You don't mind?"

"Of course I don't mind," she said. "You *are* Jules's cousin, after all. Speaking of which, I thought you were staying with his family for the time being. What are you doing over here?"

"I'm doing research on a paper for my Applied Necromancy class for extra credit," he explained, looking sheepish. "I know, I know: I'm a *complete* spod. Jules already said so."

"There's nothing wrong with that," Lilith lied as she sat down opposite him.

Xander set the document tube he was carrying

down on the table and then glanced over at the partially unrolled scroll Lilith was attempting to read.

"Did you specifically ask for that text?"

"No, the scrivener guy pulled it."

"You mean Clovis?" Xander chuckled. "He's an excellent scrivener, but if you ask him what time it is, he'll give you a scroll on watchmaking. You're better off with *The Apprentice Alchemist's Guide*, by Skorzeny. It's a lot easier to understand."

"Thanks, Exo," Lilith said, now focusing the full force of her smile on him. "You're *really* smart, you know that?"

"Yeah, well," he mumbled, dropping his gaze as he blushed.

"Jules told me you help him with *his* alchemy homework. Do you think you could help me, too?"

Xander blinked in surprise and looked around, as if uncertain Lilith was talking to him. "You want *me* to tutor you?"

"Yes."

"Are you sure about that? I mean, this isn't a joke or anything?"

Lilith leaned forward, her face a mask of seriousness. "Does it *look* like I'm joking?"

"No," he admitted, "but I thought you, you know, didn't like me."

"You're being silly again, Exo!" Lilith laughed. "Of *course* I like you. Whatever gave you the idea I didn't?"

"I dunno." He shrugged. "Maybe it was all those times you called me creepy and told me to go away when we were growing up."

"We were just kids!" Lilith insisted. "Things have changed since then."

"Not *that* much," Xander replied. "Look, Lilith—I'll help you with your alchemy homework, but only if you agree to make me your escort at the Grand Ball."

"Are you *crazy*?!" Lilith recoiled, her voice rising so sharply it threatened to enter the ultrasonic register. Several other patrons of the scrivenery paused to look up from their research and scowl in the direction of the two fledglings.

"Okay, if you don't want my help . . . It's your decision." Xander started gathering up his things.

"It's not that!" Lilith lied again. "It's just that the Grand Ball is this weekend and I already asked Barnabas Barlow to be my escort."

"I understand," Xander said, getting to his feet. "But those are my terms; take 'em or leave 'em."

"All right! You win!" Lilith said, trying her best to mask her disgust. "You're my escort."

Xander smiled and held out his hand. "It's a deal, then?"

"Deal," Lilith agreed, suppressing a shudder.

Jules de Laval reclined against the padded leather headboard of his king-size bed, idly fingering the keyboard of his Guitar Hero controller as the video game played on the fifty-inch plasma flat screen mounted on the ceiling overhead.

He hadn't heard from Lilith all night, and she hadn't shown up at the club. He wondered if she'd found out about Carmen. No, then he *definitely* would have heard from her. Besides, Carmen had been at the Belfry, and she didn't seem a bit scared or missing any body parts, so obviously Lilith couldn't know about their affair, at least not yet.

She needed to find out pretty soon, though, because Carmen was starting to really get on his nerves. Every time Ollie got up to get a round of drinks or hit the john, she was all over Jules, squeezing the inside of his thigh and rubbing her boobs against his arms and chest. He'd enjoyed it the first few weeks, but no more. It was time for Lilith to figure out what was going on and chase Carmen off.

Carmen had been way too easy, in every sense of the word. She was so desperate to live Lilith's life second-hand, he'd barely had to pursue her in the first place. Carmen already wore the same designers, makeup, and perfume as Lilith, so she had jumped at the chance to sleep with Lilith's boyfriend as well.

Once the truth came out about Carmen, the affair would have served its purpose, which was to make Lilith insecure and force her to focus her attention exclusively on him. Recently she had become even more self-absorbed and distant than usual. Jules suspected that she was seeing someone on the side, but appearing jealous would give her the upper hand, and he was determined to avoid that. It was better that she be the one out of control while he remained calm and collected. He needed her just as much as she needed him, but he would gladly burn before admitting it.

Yes, it was definitely time for Carmen to join the ranks of the other disgraced BFFs Lilith had jettisoned from her inner circle for trying to steal her boyfriend. Once Lilith's attention waned, as it always did, he would take up with another girl. And this time he had a far more challenging conquest in his sights.

Cally wasn't a part of Lilith's clique. In fact, Jules had never seen Lilith hate anyone like she hated the New Blood, not even the Maledetto sisters, whose family had a sworn vendetta against her own. The potential payoff for successfully seducing Cally might very well be keeping Lilith safely under his thumb forever. And maybe, this time, he would also keep Cally around after the fact. Perhaps that harem idea of Sergei's wasn't so crazy after all. . . .

"Hey, cuz—you busy?"

Jules glanced up as his cousin Xander stuck his head into the room. "Nah, not really." He shrugged, hitting pause on the game. "S'up, dude?"

"I, uh, just got back from the Central Scrivenery, and I thought I ought to tell you first before you heard it from someone else. . . ."

"Tell me what?" Jules frowned.

"Well, while I was doing research at the scrivenery, I ran into this girl I know. And one thing led to another, and, well, she asked me to be her escort for the Grand Ball."

"Congratulations, Exo!" Jules grinned. "I told you not to give up hope! Who's the lucky deb? Is it that Usher chick?"

"Nooo," Xander said uneasily, rubbing the back of his neck. "It's not her."

"Who is it, then? Don't keep me guessing. It's got to be one of the spods from Bathory if you ran into her at the Central Scrivenery, right?"

"Not necessarily," Xander said defensively. "A lot of people besides spods use the Central Scrivenery."

"Oh, yeah?" Jules smirked. "Like who?"

"Like Lilith."

The game controller dropped from Jules's hands as if his fingers had suddenly turned to stone. "You're shitting me."

"Urlok as my witness, Lilith was there. And she asked me to be her escort."

"You're tripping, right?" Jules said, getting to his feet. "I mean, there is *no way* Lilith would *ever* set foot inside the Central Scrivenery. And I *know* she already had an escort lined up for the Grand Ball: Barnabas Barlow, the captain of Ruthven's flight team."

"Not anymore," Xander said with a sly grin.

"What did you do to Lilith to make her pick you over Barlow?" Jules asked suspiciously. "Did you put a charm on her?"

"I would never use sorcery on a fellow vampire," Xander replied, a wounded look on his face. "You know me better than that. Is it *that* incredible to you that Lilith would change her mind in favor of me?"

"You want me to be honest? *Yes!* And you know it, Xander! So what did you do?"

"If you *must* know, I kind of, uh, used extortion. She wanted me to help her with her alchemy homework for the rest of the school year. I told her I'd do it but only if she let me be her escort."

"Blood of the Founders!" Jules snarled. "Lilith was right about you after all. You *do* have the hots for her!"

"Jules, everything with a pulse has the hots for Lilith! That's never bothered you before." Xander shook his head in amazement. "Besides, I thought you'd be relieved that Barlow wouldn't be her escort. The jerk's middle name is practically 'Date Rape.'"

"Barlow isn't my *friend*!" Jules responded heatedly. "You are."

"It's not like you could escort her yourself, anyway. If I didn't know better, I'd say you were jealous."

"Jealous?" Jules snorted derisively. "What do I have to be jealous of?"

"If you're not jealous, then why are you acting like this? I thought you might be surprised by the news, but I didn't think you'd be angry."

"I thought I could trust you, Xander," Jules replied sullenly.

"Trust? Ha! That's a good one, coming from you," Xander said with a humorless laugh. "You're the one who's always fooling around behind Lilith's back."

"That has nothing to do with this, and you know it," Jules snapped. "Now get on the phone and call her and tell her you changed your mind."

"What?"

"Tell her you're not going to tutor her and she can go to the Grand Ball with Barlow instead."

"Jules, if I don't help her with her studies, she's gonna flunk out. Is that what you really want?"

"I don't care if she flunks or not! I just want you to stay away from her!"

Xander fixed his cousin with a black stare, the last hint of affability draining from his face and voice. "It's because I'm an Orlock, isn't it? I thought you at least were different, but Uncle Vanya was right: you de Lavals are all the same. You can't accept the fact that Dad didn't have to use a potion or a charm or a spell on Mom to make her marry him. Still, that doesn't keep your family from coveting the Orlock bloodright and wealth, does it?"

"Exo, wait—you've got it all wrong," Jules said, placing a hand on his cousin's shoulder, only to have Xander shrug it off. "You know me better than that. . . ."

"That's the trouble, Jules, I *do* know you," Xander replied icily. Reaching inside his book bag with his spidery fingers, he tossed a parchment scroll onto the foot of Jules's bed. "There's your homework assignment for Professor Frid's alchemy class. From now on, you're on your own. I wouldn't bother buying a new snowboard for Vail if I were you."

"Exo! C'mon, cuz! Don't do me like that." Jules laughed nervously, trying to fight the panic rising in his gut as Xander turned and headed out the door.

"See you at the Grand Ball," Xander replied, shutting the bedroom door behind him without a backward glance.

CHAPTER FIFTEEN

"Cally! Hurry up!" Sheila Monture shouted down the hall to her daughter. "Your date should be here any minute."

Cally emerged from the bathroom, blotting her lipstick on a folded piece of toilet paper. "Baron Metzger's not my date, Mom—he's supposed to be my father!"

"You know what I mean," Sheila replied. "Just hurry up and finish your makeup so I can take your picture in the living room."

"Mom!" Cally said, rolling her eyes in exasperation.

"What?" Sheila said as she loaded the film into her Polaroid camera. "A mother can't take a photo of her only daughter before she leaves for her debutante ball?"

"A *vampire* mother can't!"

"Well, for once I'm glad I'm not one of them," Sheila

replied. "Although I *do* wish I could go with you." Sheila glanced over at the framed picture of her late parents, which sat on a bookshelf in the living room. "It's a shame your grandparents weren't here for this."

Cally wrinkled her nose and raised an eyebrow. "Somehow I don't think Granny would have liked the idea of my being a debutante at the Rauhnacht Ball."

"Your grandfather certainly wouldn't have. But even though your grandmother tried to raise you outside vampire culture as much as possible, she knew there would come a time when you would have to choose. And she would have loved you no matter how you decided to live your life." She took a deep, hitching breath and looked into her daughter's eyes. "Cally, I know I've made a lot of mistakes . . . but you were *never* one of them. I realize I'm not the kind of mother a girl like you should be proud of, but a moment hasn't gone by since you were born that *I* haven't been proud of *you.*"

Cally blinked rapidly. "Mom, you're going to make me ruin my makeup!" she said with a choked little half laugh as she fanned at her eyes.

"Oh! I'm sorry, sweetie," Sheila said apologetically. "I'll go fetch a tissue—*put that back!*" Sheila abruptly hurried across the living room and snatched a framed photograph out of Walther's hands and pressed it protectively against her breasts. "That does *not* get packed with the rest of the bric-a-brac!

It travels with *me* and no one else!"

The undead stared as if she was speaking Urdu and moved to reclaim the photograph.

"Cally!" Sheila yelled over her shoulder, a fearful look on her face. "Tell him to leave me alone."

"Walther!" Cally shouted at the undead as if he was a dog scooting on the rug. "My mother will take care of the photograph. Go help Sinclair prepare for the movers."

"As you wish, young mistress," Walther replied.

Cally shook her head as she watched the undead servant walk out of the room. Although they gave her the creeps, she had to admit they had their uses. They had already managed to pack almost everything in the apartment. She stared at the cardboard boxes neatly lined against the wall: their life in Williamsburg, ready to be packed into a nondescript moving van and driven to the docks, where they would be loaded on a freighter headed for the Baltic Sea.

"Okay, say B negative!" Sheila said, pointing the Polaroid at her daughter.

Cally forced the corners of her mouth up in an approximation of a smile as her mother snapped her picture. Suddenly the door buzzer sounded.

"Oh! That's him!" Sheila said excitedly. She waved the still-developing Polaroid like a Southern belle having the vapors at her spring cotillion. "Quick! Get your wrap. And your purse. And don't forget your invitation! You'll have to show that to the major domo once you arrive."

"Stop freaking out; I've got everything, Mom," Cally said, holding up her purse and invitation so Sheila could see them. "*Please*, you've got to go to your room now."

Sheila nodded her understanding and grudgingly headed down the hallway. She turned to give her daughter a sad little smile.

"You'll be careful, won't you, baby? Stay away from Lilith as much as you can, okay?"

"I intend to. Besides, she kept her distance the last few nights, so I'm not expecting a lot of trouble from her tonight," Cally assured her. Of course, she had made a point of not telling her mother that her escort was Lilith's boyfriend. She didn't view it as lying as much as keeping Sheila from freaking out. "I'll meet you at JFK when it's over and tell you *all* about it."

"And don't leave out the juicy stuff!" Sheila laughed as she closed the door of her bedroom behind her.

Satisfied her mother was safely out of sight, Cally hurried to answer the door as fast as her high heels permitted.

"Welcome to our home, Baron Metzger."

Standing six foot four, with shoulders as broad as those of a linebacker, Baron Karl Metzger looked every inch the European nobleman. Appearing to be in his early fifties, his chiseled features were accentuated by steel-gray hair that he wore brushed back from his broad forehead like a lion's mane.

"Good evening, Miss Monture," he said, his voice a velvety baritone. "Your father was right—you are a *most* striking young lady. That is a lovely gown you are wearing, my dear!" Baron Metzger eyed the black off-the-shoulder charmeuse gown with its A-line skirt, pleated bust, and ruby brooch. "Where did you get it?"

"I made it myself," Cally admitted with a shy smile.

"Indeed?" Baron Metzger's eyebrow came up even farther. "Your father said you were beautiful, but he said nothing of you being gifted as well. I know a thing or two about fashion. Once you are safely away from New York, I shall make a point of introducing you to my business partner, Nazaire."

Cally gasped in surprise. "You mean the designer, Nazaire d'Ombres? He's one of you—I mean, us?"

Baron Metzger nodded. "Indeed he is. He could definitely use input from someone like you right now!"

"That would be *incredible*!" Cally said, barely able to contain her excitement. "Thank you, Baron Metzger! Oh, and thank you for pretending to be my dad, too."

Baron Metzger bowed his head, placing a hand over his heart. "As vassal to your father, I am his to command."

"You work for my dad?"

"In a way. I swore fealty to your grandfather, Adolphus Todesking, nearly four hundred years ago, after he defeated my father, Kurt, and usurped the Metzger bloodright. I am now eternally bound to his descendants."

"Oh," Cally said, her smile suddenly losing some of its previous sparkle. If there was anything more disconcerting than being waited on by the undead, who were humans her ancestors had more or less murdered, it was pretending a former enemy was her father.

"Come, my dear, it's time we go. We still have a lengthy drive out to Count Orlock's estate."

"Yes, Baron," Cally replied, gathering up her things.

"My, you *are* a polite child for this day and age," Baron Metzger said approvingly. "But from here on, perhaps it would be wiser if you called me Father."

When she heard the door shut behind Cally, Sheila Monture returned to the living room and sat on the chaise lounge while Walther and Sinclair disassembled her bedroom suite and prepared it for transatlantic shipping and storage. She reached underneath the chaise's red velvet skirting, pulled out a half-empty bottle of Ancient Age, and started drinking. The flat-screen TV and home theater system were already wrapped in layers of bubble wrap, awaiting the arrival of the movers. Tonight she'd be content to look at the photo of her parents she had rescued from Walther.

"I'm sorry, Daddy," Sheila said. "I wish you knew that." The tears trickling down her face mingled with the bourbon, giving it a mildly salty taste.

As she raised the bottle again, Sheila heard a muffled ringing sound. It seemed to be coming from Cally's room.

A cell phone? Since when did Cally have a cell phone? Sheila got to her feet and headed, somewhat unsteadily, for her daughter's bedroom, where she found a small silver phone lying forgotten, buried under the rumpled sheets of the canopy bed.

Sheila stared at the caller ID, trying to see who it was, but the incoming caller's identity was blocked. She flipped open the phone and put the receiver to her ear.

"Cally, thank God I reached you in time!" a young male voice said breathlessly. "You have to believe me—I never intended for it to end like this! Please forgive me. I was so afraid I was going to lose you forever! Don't hang up. Please . . . I know you don't want to talk to me, but you've *got* to listen!"

"Who is this?" Sheila scowled.

"Cally?" The timbre of the young man's voice suddenly changed from desperate to cautious.

"This is Cally's mother, and Cally isn't here," Sheila said in a stern voice. "She left to go to the Grand Ball with Baron Metz—I mean, her father."

"God, no—!" The young man gasped. "You've got to stop them, Ms. Monture! You've got to reach her and tell her not to go!"

"I know who you are!" Sheila said in sudden

realization. "You're that no-good Maledetto boy. You've got some nerve calling here. Leave my daughter alone! She doesn't need to get mixed up with a bunch of two-bit killers."

"Sheila! Please, you don't understand—!" The young man's voice was close to panic. "You're *both* in danger! You *have* to get out of the house!"

"How do you know my name?" Sheila frowned. "Go away and leave my baby alone, you hear me? She doesn't need you complicating her life!" She snapped the cell phone shut and tossed it back onto the bed. As she stepped out of her daughter's room, there was a loud, booming knock on the front door, followed by a second, even louder one. No doubt it was the movers come to collect their things.

"Hold your horses, I'm coming!" Sheila yelled. Whoever was on the other side of the door sounded like they were using a battering ram instead of their fists. "There's no need to knock the door off its hinges—!"

Although she had not been raised in vampire society, Cally knew that Rauhnacht was one of a handful of dates held sacred by her father's people. Throughout the world, Old Bloods and New Bloods alike were gathered that night to welcome the arrival of the Dark Season, where the nights are longer than the days, as they had done for thousands of years.

Scores of prominent Old Bloods had traveled from

as far as half a world away to view the newest crop of young females at the palatial home of Count Boris Orlock.

Situated at the end of a two-mile-long driveway, King's Stone seemed to rise like some great leviathan from the nearby Atlantic Ocean. The four stone towers of the modern-day castle stood watch over the cardinal points of the compass. As Baron Metzger's vintage Duesenberg wended its way along the Orlocks' private drive, Cally spotted a topiary garden. At first she smiled at the sight of the shrubbery clipped to resemble animals and mythic beasts—then she realized that the topiary animals were divided into predator and prey. An arborvitae lion stalked a bay laurel gazelle, while a myrtle wolf hunted a sheep sculpted of yew, and a dragon made of holly brought down a boxwood pig.

As Cally stared at the grim tableaux, something white flashed at the corner of her eye and she turned her head to see what it might be. A man was staggering through the hedges, his clothes badly disheveled. He was wildly waving a white cane with a red tip.

"*Help me!*" the blind man cried in terror. "For the love of all that's holy, *somebody please help me*!"

A gang of small children swarmed out from behind the topiary wolf, giggling and laughing as if on a McDonald's playground. As one, they surged forward and took the blind man to the ground. Cally quickly looked away as they snapped at their struggling prey with their razor-sharp baby fangs.

"Ahhh, blindman's bluff!" Baron Metzger said with a nostalgic smile. "To be young and innocent again!"

As the baron's car entered the cobblestone courtyard, an undead servant dressed in the livery of a footman hurried forward and opened the passenger door for Cally.

Baron Metzger took her hand and wrapped it around his arm, and together they began to climb the entry stairs of King's Stone. Cally looked up and glimpsed what appeared to be a gargoyle perched high atop the conical roof of the north tower.

The Orlocks' major domo, a bald man with a Prussian accent and a dueling scar, stood guard in the foyer, checking the credentials of all who entered his master's home. Cally handed him her invitation, which he took and added to a pile on the table beside him.

"Welcome to King's Stone," the head butler said. "The guests are gathered in the Grand Hall."

As Cally and Baron Metzger walked forward, a pair of servants in Orlock livery opened the large double doors at the other end of the room. Cally gasped in awe at the sight of the Grand Hall spread before her. It was thirty-five feet wide and seventy feet long, with a vaulted ceiling that rose to the third floor. The walls of the great hall were lined with red damask and draped with tapestries dating back to the twelfth century. Gathered within its vast space were nearly three hundred vampires, chatting and laughing among themselves as they sampled the blood gushing from solid-gold heated beverage fountains, one for each blood type, arrayed along a medieval banquet table that stretched half the length of the room.

"Come, my dear," Baron Metzger said. "We must pay our respects to King's Stone's lord and lady. Ah! There they are!" He raised a hand in greeting. "Boris!"

On hearing his name, the master of King's Stone turned to greet his old friend.

Cally had heard of Orlocks since she was a kid—she had even met one, the count's own son, Xander—but nothing had prepared her for this.

Standing nearly seven feet tall despite the hump in his back, Count Boris Orlock—heir to the bloodright of Urlok the Terrible, greatest of all the Founders—looked like a ghastly amalgamation of skull, bat, and spider. He was cadaverously thin, with a completely hair-less head and fanged front teeth that stuck out of his oddly sensuous mouth like tiny knitting needles. His ears were unnaturally large and pointed, like those of a bat, with clumps of wiry hair growing out of them like weeds. He held his long, spindly arms tucked in close to his body and compulsively dry-washed his hands, the fingers of which were as long and gnarled as the legs of a king crab. Yet despite his frightful appearance, the count possessed an oddly dignified hideousness that is only found in those as powerful as they are ugly. He commanded respect as well as repugnance from those around him.

"Karl! How good to see you, old friend!" Count Orlock smiled, looking like a hairless rat baring its fangs as he warmly clasped his guest's hand in his own.

"It is equally good to see you, dear Boris! And Countess—you are as lovely as ever."

Where her husband was the very definition of the word *nightmare*, Countess Juliana Orlock was a dream made flesh. With her perfect skin, sapphire-blue eyes, long platinum hair, and glamorous, shimmering sequined one-shoulder gown, she looked like she should be on her way to a Hollywood premiere, not a vampire ball.

"Ah, Baron—still the silver-tongued devil, I see," she said fondly.

"Come now, Juliana." Count Orlock smiled, gently stroking one of his outlandishly long fingers against his wife's flawless cheek. "You cannot fault a man for simply stating a fact."

"Dearest, you're making me blush," the countess said with a coy smile.

"Your Illustriousness, I would like to introduce you to my daughter, Miss Cally Monture."

Count Orlock smiled, taking Cally's hand in his monstrous one. To her surprise, his touch was incredibly delicate. "I was not aware you *had* a daughter, Karl."

"Her mother was one of my New Blood concubines,"

Baron Metzger explained. "I have chosen to acknowledge Cally now that my dear wife is no longer with us.".

"Ah!" Count Orlock said with knowing nod. "She is *exquisite*, Karl."

"You're too kind, Count," Cally said. She curtsied.

"Enough chitchatting with old fossils such as myself!" Count Orlock laughed. "It's Rauhnacht! Tonight is for the young! I'll have one of my pages take you upstairs to where the other debutantes are. It won't be long before the ceremony begins."

CHAPTER SIXTEEN

The room where the debutantes waited for their presentation at the Grand Ball was on the third floor
of the main section of King's Stone. As she was
escorted down the gloomy corridor, Cally noticed that
the sconces that lined them were carved to resemble
forearms, the gnarled hands holding lit candles. The
servant stopped and opened a diamond-paneled oak
door, revealing an opulently appointed salon decorated
in the Louis XIV style. As she scanned the room for
her friends, Cally recognized many of the girls from
Bathory—but there were several she had never seen
before, like the girl in the black sari-style Versace gown
and the dark-haired girl in the Rei Kawakubo original.

The Maledetto twins and Melinda were clustered
in a corner of the salon, as far away from Lilith's clique
as possible. Bella and Bette sat facing each other on

an antique figure-eight love seat, making last-minute adjustments to their hair and makeup. For the first time since she'd known them, the twins were wearing their hair unbound and were dressed differently. Melinda sat in a nearby chair, swapping out a pair of Manolo platform slingbacks in favor of a pair of Jimmy Choo strappies.

Cally automatically started across the room toward the other girls, only to stop halfway. As much as she wanted to be with her friends on her last night in New York, she could not go against her father's wishes.

An older woman, dressed in a strapless evening gown so tight it seemed to be pushing her breasts into her face, suddenly appeared in front of Cally. "You're late! The presentation ceremony is less than an hour away. Which one are you?" she asked, peering around her bust at the new arrival.

"Cally Monture."

The older woman consulted the PDA she held in one hand, stabbing at the display with her stylus. "Monture . . . Monture . . . Ah! Here you are. My name is Pandora Grume; I have been assigned to make sure everyone and everything runs on time tonight."

"What is *she* doing here?" Lilith Todd, dressed in a black Marchesa satin chiffon sculpted evening gown, stood glaring at Cally, her hands planted firmly on her hips as she tapped a Prada-shod foot in anger. "Since when does the Presentation Committee extend invitations to fatherless *bastards*?"

The entire room fell silent and everyone, including Melinda and the twins, turned to stare at Cally.

"I *have* a father," Cally replied, trying to remain calm.

"Yeah, but you don't even know his name!" Carmen said, getting up from a nearby sofa. "Lilith told me so!"

"That's not true anymore," Cally said, addressing Carmen while keeping an eye on Lilith. "My father has claimed me as his legal daughter."

On hearing this, Lilith flinched and fell silent. Carmen, however, continued to press her verbal attack. "Oh, yeah? Who is he, then?"

"Baron Metzger."

"Metzger?" Lilith said in a tight voice, her eyes narrowing into suspicious slits.

"May I have your attention?" Madame Grume said, her voice cutting right through the giggly chatter that filled the room. "It's time for the debutantes to claim their bouquets." She stepped aside as an Orlock family footman entered, pushing a large serving cart containing a baker's dozen of bouquets.

Although the bouquets were all fashioned from roses, they were far from identical. Each was unique and had a card affixed to it, identifying which girl it was for and the escort it was from.

Lilith stepped forward, claiming her place at the head of the line. She was pleasantly surprised to discover that her bouquet was the nicest one on the cart: six bright red Passion roses decorated with delicate stems of twisted willow and bound in black satin. Exo might be a spod and a bat boy, but at least he had great taste. As she picked up her bouquet, she spotted Cally's name written on a card attached to a bunch of velvety dark-red Black Magic roses, their stems bound in antique lace.

She wondered what kind of pathetic loser would agree to be the escort of a half-blood bastard like Monture. Deciding it would be good for a chuckle, she flipped the card over—only to stare, dumbstruck, at the name on the other side.

It had to be a mistake. It *couldn't* be. He *wouldn't*. He *knew* how she felt about Cally! Lilith's heart began to vibrate in her chest until she feared it would tear itself loose.

"Is something wrong, Lili?" Carmen asked. "Your hands are shaking."

Lilith grabbed her bouquet and ran out of the room, leaving Carmen to stare after her, perplexed. The redhead claimed her own bouquet—a half dozen deep crimson roses decorated with Swarovski crystals—and hurried after her friend.

Carmen found Lilith in the powder room across the hall from the salon. She was standing in front of the sink, running the hot water until steam rose from the basin. As Carmen watched, Lilith thrust her hands under the scalding torrent, hissing through her teeth as her skin turned bright red and blisters rose across her palms.

"What are you doing?" Carmen gasped.

"I'm not going to cry," Lilith said between gritted teeth as she stepped away from the sink. "I *refuse* to ruin my makeup. Not in front of *her*."

The burns she had inflicted on herself were already starting to fade, along with the pain that accompanied them. She had come dangerously close to losing control in front of the others, but plunging her hands into scalding water had driven the tears from her eyes.

"What are you talking about?" Carmen frowned.

"It's about Jules."

"What about him?" Carmen asked uneasily, wondering if rumors had finally reached Lilith's ears.

"He's Cally's escort!" Lilith spat.

Carmen's relief that her affair with Jules had not been discovered was engulfed by jealousy of her own, which she quickly masked as outrage on Lilith's behalf. "That *bitch*! How *dare* she! I'm going to give her a piece of my mind!" As she stormed out of the powder room and back into the salon, her hands clenched into angry fists, Carmen remembered the look on Jules's face the night he'd told her he didn't want to be her escort.

That son of a bitch! she thought. *He turns* me *down*

but doesn't have any problem saying yes to some New Blood slut!

Cally was sitting alone on a love seat when Carmen Duivel stomped across the room, her emerald-green eyes ablaze with anger.

"That was a *really* shitty thing to do to Lilith!" Carmen said hotly.

"I have no idea what you're talking about," Cally replied.

"Don't hand me that!" Carmen nearly shouted. "You know *exactly* what I mean. You're trying to steal Jules away from Lilith!"

"Are you nuts?" Cally eyed Carmen like she would a street crazy ranting on the subway platform. "He's merely acting as my escort, nothing else. I asked him and he said yes. Besides, I'm not the one *fucking* him," she said pointedly.

Carmen's jealous anger was abruptly replaced by a tight knot in her belly. "What do you mean by that?"

"What do you *think* I mean?" Cally snapped. "I have nothing to be ashamed of. *I'm* not the one claiming to be Lilith's friend."

Carmen glanced about uneasily. Every eye and ear in the room was now trained on her. Suddenly using Lilith as an excuse to confront Cally about Jules didn't seem like such a good idea.

Unable to come up with a catty remark that wouldn't

get her in even deeper trouble, Carmen simply walked off. As she did, she saw Lilith standing in the doorway of the salon, watching her with cold, hard eyes.

"Lilith, it's not what it sounds like," Carmen assured her.

Lilith said nothing as she stepped around the redhead. As Carmen moved to follow her, Lilith turned around and fixed her with a hard glare.

"*No.*"

"But—"

"I *said* no." Lilith stalked across the room to join Lula and Armida. Carmen couldn't process the speed with which she had just fallen from grace. On what was supposed to be her official introduction to Old Blood society, Carmen's social life had just been cut off, as cleanly and completely as a diseased limb severed by a surgeon.

As Carmen wandered about, forlornly trying to find somewhere to sit that was safely out of Lilith's range, the salon doors flew open and Madame Grume reentered the room in front of yet another serving cart, this one containing a cut-crystal punch bowl and thirteen matching cups. The dark red liquid in the bowl sloshed gently back and forth as the servant wheeled the cart into the middle of the room.

"You're in for a real treat! Count Orlock has

graciously selected something *very* special from his private cellars for you young ladies to enjoy," Madame Grume announced. "It's HH phenotype, the fabled Bombay blood—the rarest in the world!"

The undead servant ladled the blood into the dainty crystal cups carefully so as not to waste a single drop of the precious vintage. Then he handed them out one by one to the assembled girls.

"Praise to the Founders," Madame Grume intoned.

"To the Founders," the girls said in unison, raising their drinks in a toast.

Cally sipped the blood, which was far more impressive than anything she'd ever tasted in her life. So *this* was how the mega-rich Old Bloods lived.

She was so busy enjoying her drink, she hadn't noticed that Lilith was standing near her.

"Watch your elbow!" Lilith snapped, jostling Cally's arm.

There was a collective gasp as the drink spilled from the punch cup onto the skirt of Cally's dress. The thick blood left an oil slick–style stain on the dark fabric.

"My dress!" Cally wailed.

"It's not *my* fault you got in my way!"

The sight of Lilith's sneering face made Cally so mad her whole body seemed to vibrate. "You did that on purpose!"

"How dare you accuse me of such a thing!" Lilith

sniffed indignantly. "If you hadn't been such a klutz, you wouldn't have spilled anything to begin with!"

"Take that back!"

"Oh, yeah? Who's gonna make me?"

To Cally's surprise, Bella and Bette Maledetto stepped forward, flanking her on either side.

"Take it back, Lilith," Bella said sternly.

"Yeah, leave her alone," Bette agreed.

Lilith automatically glanced over her shoulder, only to remember she could no longer count on Carmen to back her up. She looked over to Armida and Lula, who were watching from the sidelines. Before Lilith could make eye contact, both girls quickly looked away.

"What's the matter, Lilith?" Melinda asked, moving to join her friends. "Cat got your tongue?"

Lilith glared and opened her mouth, only to suddenly change her mind and walk away without another word. The four friends exchanged glances with one another as they shared a single sigh of relief.

"I can't believe you guys were willing to do that after the way I've treated you," Cally said in amazement.

"You and Melinda are the only girls at Bathory who have ever treated us decently," Bette said. "You're the only real friends we've ever had."

"My sister's right." Bella nodded. "Nothing can change the fondness we have for you, Cally."

Cally shook her head, humbled by the show of loyalty

the twins had displayed on her behalf. How could she have allowed Victor Todd, who was little more than a stranger, to manipulate her into severing ties with her best friends? As much as she wanted to be a part of her father's world, Cally decided there were limits to how far she would go to please him.

"I don't care if it gets me in trouble or not, I'm going to hang out with whoever I want to from now on," Cally said. "And if my parents don't like it—well, they'll just have to get used to it."

Besides, Cally told herself, what difference should it make to her father if she spent the evening hanging out with her friends one last time? Since she was being forced to change her entire world on short notice, it seemed only fair to her that she get to enjoy the last night of her old life in the company of her friends.

"I'm so proud of you two," Cally said. "You both look fantastic!"

"I *love* your dress!" Bette said enthusiastically.

"Me too!" Bella agreed, and then grimaced. "Sorry about it being ruined."

"We'll just see about that," Melinda said, steering Cally over to a nearby chair. "I have something that should fix things," she explained, taking a small green bottle and a handkerchief from her clutch purse. "It's a special formula handed down from my mother's side of the family, designed to eradicate all traces of a stain without harming the fabric. I never go anywhere without it in case of 'accidents.'" She removed the stopper from the bottle and wet the hanky, then proceeded to daub at the blood on Cally's skirt. "See? It's coming out perfectly. . . ."

"Thanks, Melly," Cally said. "I really appreciate this."

"It's the least I can do under the circumstances." Melinda shrugged. "I never really thanked you for what you did the other night."

"What? You mean the pier? Forget about it."

"Forget that I owe you a blood debt? Not likely. I owe you my life." She leaned in and whispered: "And so does my friend. His name's Tommy Bang. No jokes, please. His father runs the Ghost Tigers down in Chinatown."

"You don't owe me anything, Melly," Cally said. "You would have done the same if our positions had been reversed."

"I hope I get a chance to find out—not that I'm counting on you being ambushed by Van Helsings."

"At least not anytime soon." Cally laughed.

"Okay, young ladies, your time is almost at hand!" Madame Grume announced. "I need you to line up in order in the hallway. Single file! And don't forget your bouquets! Follow me." The debutantes gathered their things and went out into the hallway, while Madame

Grume checked her PDA. "Who's first? Let me see . . .
Armida Aitken?"

"Here," Armida said, raising her hand.

"And your escort is . . . ?"

"Erik Geist."

"Armida, I need you to go stand in front of that door
at the end of the hall. When it opens and you hear
your name called, you are to step over the threshold.
On the other side is the top of the staircase. Your father
will be there waiting for you. You will give him your
right hand while holding your bouquet with your left,
then you will be led down the stairs. At the foot of the
staircase your escort, young Mr. Geist, will be waiting
for you.

"He will then take you by the right hand and squire
you around the ballroom. You will curtsy at the four
points and then make your fifth and final curtsy to
the host and hostess of the Grand Ball. Once you have
finished, you and Mr. Geist will retire to the platform
on the far side of the ballroom, where you will sit on
one of the chairs while your escort stands behind you.
You will then wait for the rest of the young ladies to
make their debuts. The presentation of the thirteenth
and final debutante will signal the first waltz of the
Grand Ball.

"Once the first waltz begins, you will leave your
bouquet on your chair and move onto the dance floor

with your escort. The whole presentation process, from start to finish, shouldn't take any more than five minutes. Do you understand that, dear?"

Armida nodded. "I wait until the door opens and I hear my name called."

Madame Grume heaved a sigh. "Close enough, dear."

As she awaited her turn, Cally was relieved to find herself grouped with Melinda and the twins instead of sandwiched between strangers or, even more likely, enemies. After the Maledetto sisters stepped through the doorway to be escorted down the staircase by their father, Melinda leaned in close and said in a low voice: "I'm to tell you that you now have friends in Chinatown."

"It's always good to have friends."

"*Especially* if you keep insisting on antagonizing Lilith." Melinda shook her head in disbelief. "Jules as an escort? Girl, what were you thinking?"

"I was thinking Lilith can kiss my ass."

As the two friends collapsed into giggles, Cally realized that this would be a moment she would remember for the rest of her life, however long that life might be. As much as she enjoyed being with Melinda and the twins, the fun she was having with them was equally mixed with sadness.

Cally felt her secrets—*all* of them—scrambling up

her throat, clamoring against one another in their hurry to leap from her lips. She dug her nails into the palms of her hands, hoping the pain would drive away the compulsion to come clean, but it was no good.

"Melly, there's something important I have to tell you. . . ."

"What is it?"

Before Cally could say anything more, Madame Grume tapped Melinda on the shoulder. "Miss Mauvais! You're next!"

Melinda glanced up at Cally anxiously. "How do I look?"

"Absolutely beautiful, Melly," Cally said.

Melinda stepped toward the door, holding her bouquet close to her midriff with both hands. She suddenly frowned and looked back at Cally. "What was it you needed to tell me?"

"Thanks for being my friend, that's all." Cally smiled.

Before Melinda could reply, the door swung open and a voice on the other side boomed out: "Anton Mauvais of Manhattan presents to you his daughter: Melinda."

Cally heaved a tiny sigh of relief as Melinda stepped through the door. Although she knew she had just narrowly avoided disaster, part of her was sad that she hadn't had time to tell the truth.

It seemed no matter how close she got to others, she always had to keep those she cared for at arm's length. And no matter what kind of spin her father put on it, being unable to tell your friend good-bye really, really sucked.

CHAPTER SEVENTEEN

"You're the Monture girl, aren't you?" Madame Grume asked.

"Yes, ma'am," Cally replied.

"Is there something wrong with your hand, dear?"

"My hand?" Cally looked down and saw that, without realizing it, she had been rubbing her left palm against the skirt of her gown. Her hand felt as if it had fallen asleep and was just starting to wake up. "It's nothing," she said quickly. "Just nerves, that's all."

"Let me assure you, you have nothing to be nervous about, child." Madame Grume smiled as she patted her on the shoulder. "You look positively ravishing!"

Suddenly the door swung open and a masculine voice intoned: "Baron Karl Metzger of Berlin and Paris presents to you his daughter: Cally Monture."

Clutching her bouquet as if it were a lifeline in a

choppy sea, Cally stepped through the doorway to find herself standing at the top of a gracefully curved thirty-foot-tall marble staircase wrapped in lengths of decorative ivy.

Below her was a massive Gothic ballroom with a vaulted ceiling of carved limestone and arched windows that looked out onto the vast grounds of the estate. Renaissance tapestries were hung in between the huge metal chandeliers. The floor of the ballroom was crowded by the same partygoers she had seen in the Grand Hall earlier, their faces turned upward, staring at her curiously. She could see people talking to one another, some behind their hands, others quite openly.

"I didn't realize he had a daughter. . . ."

"I hear she's his child by a concubine. . . ."

"What a lovely gown. . . ."

As she stared down at the cream of Old Blood society, Cally felt her knees begin to tremble and the odd tingling in her hand grew stronger, seeming to travel up her arm. She looked to her right and saw her faux father, Baron Metzger, standing on the step below her, holding out his hand.

"There's no need to be nervous, my dear," he said with a comforting smile.

Cally gratefully gave the older man her right hand while maintaining her hold on Jules's bouquet with her left. As the baron led her down the stairs, she scanned the ballroom, searching for her real father. Her smile faltered when she realized he was nowhere to be seen.

Jules was waiting at the foot of the stairs. He looked dashing in his Armani tuxedo and he eagerly stepped forward to take her hand.

"Take good care of her, young man," Baron Metzger said with a wink as he passed Cally over to her escort.

"Don't worry, sir," Jules replied. "I will."

As Cally was escorted onto the open dance floor to begin her formal introduction to the gathered socialites, the chamber quartet hidden away in the orchestra alcove began to play Mozart.

"Are you scared?" Jules asked in a stage whisper as Cally curtsied to the western point, symbolic of the setting sun.

"No, I'm not scared," Cally replied under her breath. "I'm petrified."

"Don't be." Jules led her to the eastern point, representing the rising moon. "You're doing great."

"You really think so?" Cally asked nervously. She curtsied to the southern point, which signified the dying daylight.

"Just look at them," Jules urged her as he brought her to the northern point, which represented the rising darkness.

Cally glanced up at the faces of the partygoers that ringed the dance floor. While some scowled at her in disapproval, many others were watching her with an avid interest that bordered on hunger.

"You see?" Jules smiled. "You've got them in the palm of your hand."

It was time for Cally to make her fifth and final curtsy, this time to her host and his wife. Jules led her toward the huge fireplace at the far end of the room. Seated before the hearthside in high-backed thrones with armrests adorned with ivory and bone plaques were the count and countess.

"In the name of the Founders," Count Orlock said as Cally curtsied before him, "I welcome you as one of the Blood, daughter of Metzger."

"Thank you, Your Eminence," Cally replied.

Now Jules directed her toward the raised dais on the far side of the room where her fellow debutantes sat facing the dance floor, their escorts standing behind them. Cally caught a glimpse of her father, dressed in white tie and tails, standing to one side of the staircase. He was waiting his turn to climb the steps to present Lilith. Standing next to him was a chic-looking woman dressed in a lilac crepe gown. Her blond hair was piled atop her head in a sophisticated updo, and she had the same chilly blue eyes as Lilith.

As Cally took her place on the dais with the other debutantes, she was greeted by Melinda and the twins, who were seated on matching Queen Anne chairs.

"You looked fabulous out there!"

"Thank you, Bella," Cally said.

Standing behind them were their escorts for the

evening. Cally did not recognize the young men stationed behind Bella and Bette, but she definitely knew Melinda's escort.

"Good to see you again, Cally," Lucky Maledetto said, flashing her a roguish smile.

"It's nice to see you, too," she replied, blushing ever so slightly.

"*Excuse me*, Faustus," Jules said stiffly as he stepped past Lucky.

Eyebrow cocked in amusement, Lucky watched Jules draw back Cally's chair. "Hello, Jules. I haven't seen you since Ruthven's."

"Yes, well, you know how it is," Jules replied, avoiding Lucky's gaze. "School keeps me busy."

"Of course it does," Lucky said dryly.

Cally settled into her seat, holding her bouquet in her lap. Scanning the audience, she spotted Victor Todd glowering at her from across the room, clearly displeased by her open display of friendliness toward the Maledetto family. Cally's heart flip-flopped and she quickly looked away.

Over the course of the last hour Lilith had waited impatiently as the other girls walked out the door one by one—that is, except for the Maledetto sisters, who had stepped out in tandem, flanking their father on either side as he walked them down the staircase. She had passed the time by sullenly licking the wounds dealt to her ego earlier that evening.

This was supposed to be her big night, her shining moment as the sole focus of attention at the Grand Ball, but now she discovered her father, Jules, and her supposed "best friend" had all been secretly conspiring behind her back to ruin it.

She could tell herself that it wasn't really Jules's fault. Since Cally asked him to be her escort, *she* was to blame. Of course, Jules could have turned her down—but he was weak, as all men are weak; it didn't matter if they were vampire or human. She had tolerated his occasional dalliances with the girls within their social circle. But this time he'd gone too far, even for her. She would make him pay for his callous disregard for her feelings.

She wondered if Cally genuinely believed the old baron to be her father. Lilith knew it was a lie, but did Cally? What was Victor playing at with Metzger?

And then there was the matter of Carmen. Disloyal, slutty Carmen. Compared to what her father and Jules had done, her betrayal was almost worth overlooking. *Almost.*

As she thought about how those supposedly closest to her had turned against her, Lilith's anger was replaced by a cold, calculating hatred and a desire to inflict pain and suffering on all those who had failed her. In any case, her hate kept her from succumbing to the terrible emptiness that threatened to engulf her.

She was so preoccupied with plotting the downfall of her friends and family, she almost didn't hear her name being announced. She stepped through the door and looked out across the huge room. Every eye was focused on her. She was the center of attention of over three hundred of the most influential, powerful, and privileged members of Old Blood society.

And yet . . . it was nothing compared to what she had experienced in front of the camera. One taste of pure, uncut, unqualified attention, and nothing else would do.

She found herself thinking of Kristof. No doubt he would have given his right arm to shoot a spectacle of this magnitude.

Lilith forced a smile onto her face as she took her father's hand. As Victor Todd and his daughter descended the staircase, which symbolized her transition from child to young woman, a round of applause arose from the onlookers below.

"I don't know what you think you're doing, passing your love child off as Metzger's," Lilith said through her unwavering smile. "But it's not going to do any good."

"I assure you, I had no hand in her being here," Victor replied out of the corner of his mouth. "Metzger is blackmailing me. He knows about Cally, and he has threatened to send pictures of 'Lili' to the Synod."

"What are you going to do?"

"Pay him a good deal of money, of course. He has

also demanded the right to marry into our bloodline. I have surrendered your sister to him in exchange for his silence."

"You did *what*?" she hissed, staring at her father in disbelief.

"Don't look at me, look at your audience, my dear," Victor admonished her. "Cally knows nothing of any of this—as far as she is concerned, Metzger is her father. Besides, would you have me offer you up instead?" As they reached the foot of the stairs, he whispered in her ear: "You might not believe me after all we've been through lately, but you *are* my daughter, Lilith. There is nothing I would not do to protect you, princess."

Lilith glanced out of the corner of her eye at Victor, but it was impossible to decide if he was telling the truth. As she wondered whether or not to believe her father, Xander Orlock, dressed in a Versace tuxedo, his blond hair pomaded back into a pronounced widow's peak, stepped forward and took her hand.

Xander looked up at her with deep-set blue-gray eyes, and the upper lip of his lavishly wide, sensual mouth pulled back into a smile.

"You've never looked lovelier than you do right now, Lilith," he said.

Despite herself, Lilith smiled.

Without a backward glance at her father, Lilith followed her escort onto the dance floor to make her formal curtsies to the guests. As they passed the raised platform where the other girls and their escorts were, she gave Jules a withering look. To her surprise, she saw genuine jealousy on his face—something she had never seen before.

As she observed the black looks being exchanged between the cousins, it suddenly occurred to Lilith that her means of retaliating against Jules for betraying her with her hated demi-sister was literally at her fingertips. It was all she could do to keep from grinning ear from ear. Who would ever have dreamed a spod like Exo could be so extremely useful?

While Xander squired her from west to east, south to north, Lilith made a point of smiling and pretending to enjoy his company. She watched in amusement as Xander's chest visibly puffed up with pride as he escorted the most beautiful girl in New York City around the room.

As Xander brought Lilith for her final curtsy before his parents, Lilith saw a flicker of approval in the count's eyes. However, the countess's brow was furrowed and she had a worried look on her face.

Suddenly there came the toll of the bell, ringing out the strokes of midnight. Count Orlock stood up from his throne and motioned to the orchestra.

"Rauhnacht is here at last, my friends!" Count Orlock proclaimed. "It is time for the Grand Ball to begin! And this year, the honor of the opening dance falls to none other than my own son and heir, Xander

Orlock, and his lovely companion, Miss Lilith Todd!"

As the orchestra struck up Strauss's "Vienna Blood," the young couple took to the middle of the ballroom accompanied by eager applause from the onlookers.

Lilith had expected Xander to be an awkward partner on the dance floor, but to her surprise he promptly snapped into position, taking her right hand in his left and extending her arm out to the side while his right hand slid confidently into place along the left side of her body. She could feel his hand pressing firmly against the slope of her back, just below the lower edge of her shoulder blade. She instinctively tried to put a little space between their bodies but found herself held fast.

She tossed her head back to berate him for daring to be so bold with her, only to find herself captured by his blue-gray eyes. Suddenly she no longer minded the feel of his abnormally long, yet powerful fingers against her flesh.

"Shall we dance?" Xander said with a smile.

As the future Count Orlock twirled her counterclockwise about the room, skillfully guiding her with only the slightest pressure against her waist, all her anger and schemes of vengeance fell away. Lilith found herself smiling, not because it was expected of her, but because she was actually enjoying herself.

* * *

The debutantes seated on the dais rose from their chairs and, in the company of their escorts, filed onto the dance floor, joining Xander and Lilith in their waltz. Within seconds the ballroom was filled with beautiful young girls and dashing young men in evening clothes, whirling about the dance floor like the patterns made inside a kaleidoscope.

As Cally twirled in Jules's arms, she found herself wishing she was dancing with Peter. Although the attention from Jules and Lucky was flattering—even a little bit exciting—there was no denying where her heart lay. It was a shame she could only admit this to herself now that there was no hope of her ever seeing him again.

As she and Jules wove in and around the other couples on the dance floor, it seemed to Cally as if the world was whirling around them at breakneck speed. The faces of the onlookers began to blur one into another. Then, as they twirled past one of the arched windows that looked out onto the gardens, Cally thought she glimpsed a familiar face pressed against the pane, looking in at her. With a start she recognized it as Peter's.

Her heart leaped as she craned her head about, trying to catch another glance, uncertain whether what she'd seen was real or not. But Jules was moving too fast for her to get a clear look and there were too many partygoers in the way. By the time they danced back around to the same side of the room, the window was empty.

Although she knew it had to have been an optical illusion, Cally's heart still sank in disappointment.

Of course Peter's not here, she silently chided herself. *What would he be doing here? Even if he knew where I was, it would be suicide for him to follow me.*

She told herself she needed to put Peter out of her mind. Thinking about him was making her eyes play tricks on her. Besides, there was no point in wishful thinking. Now, if only her left hand would stop tingling, she might be able to enjoy herself. . . .

Outside the ballroom, in the darkness of the cold autumn night, a lone sliver of moonlight pierced the clouds that had rolled in from the Atlantic. It fell on the gabled roofs of King's Stone and on a gargoyle perched there, with skin the color and texture of quarried rock. It lifted its broad, doglike head, sniffing the sea air with wide, flat nostrils. Off in the distance there was a brief flicker of light, followed by a low rumble.

Growling in anticipation, Talus spread his leathery wings and took to the air, eager to return to his master's side. The storm would be here soon. Very soon.

Don't miss any of the Vamp-tastic action in:

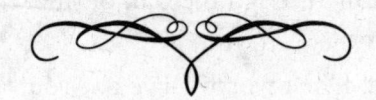

When Cally brought her goblet to her lips, she heard the sound of breaking glass from somewhere behind her. As she turned, thinking perhaps someone had dropped a drink, the windows facing the garden suddenly shattered inward. What looked like cans of shaving cream flew through the ballroom, landing on the polished floor. As one came to rest near her foot, Cally realized they weren't cans of shaving cream at all.

They were tear-gas canisters.

"Get back!" Lucky yelled, pushing Cally behind him as a dense, grayish cloud erupted into the air. "Cover your mouth!"

Within seconds the ballroom became a scene of mass chaos; the music and laughter were replaced by screams. Cally was buffeted back and forth as the guests crashed into one another trying to escape the rapidly spreading fumes. Her eyes swimming with tears, she reached out, groping blindly through the wall of smoke.

"Lucky! Where are you?"

"I'm here! Don't worry—I've got you!" he shouted, his strong hands closing around her own.

Suddenly the crowd surrounding her began to surge in the opposite direction. Cally tried to move toward Lucky, only to be wrenched from his grasp. Barely able to see and breathe, she was borne away by a living tide. Somewhere in the madness, she could hear Baron Metzger calling her name, but she could not see him, much less tell which direction his voice was coming from.

At first Lilith thought the explosions and gouts of smoke were some kind of pyrotechnic display Count Orlock had arranged for the amusement of his guests. But when her eyes started burning and her mascara began to run, she realized the fireworks had nothing to do with the Grand Ball.

"Daddy—what's going on?" she wailed.

Victor Todd took a monogrammed silk handkerchief from the breast pocket of his tuxedo and covered his nose and mouth. "We're under attack, princess!"

"Van Helsings? *Here?* They must be mad!" Irina coughed.

"Get Lilith out of here *now*," Victor said, pushing

her toward her mother.

"You heard your father," Irina said, grabbing her daughter's arm. "We've got to get out of this place!"

"Where's Jules?" Lilith looked around, but her eyes were stinging too much from the acrid smoke for her to see more than a few feet in any direction.

"The de Lavals can take care of themselves!" Irina snapped. "We've got to escape!"

"Don't tell me what to do!" Lilith said, pulling away from her mother.

"Lilith! Come back here!"

Ignoring her mother, Lilith pushed her way through the crowd. After only a few steps she quickly found herself trapped, unable to move forward or go back. As the choking fumes burned her eyes and mouth, she was overwhelmed by the urgent need to free herself from the crushing press.

"Get out of my way, damn you! I've got to get out!" she screamed, kicking and clawing at those closest to her. Those on the receiving end of Lilith's slashing nails began doing the same to those ahead of them, triggering a chain reaction.

There was a sound of smashing glass and splintering wood, immediately followed by the smell of sea air from the nearby Atlantic as the panicked partygoers pushed their way through the French doors, spilling out onto the garden terrace like hornets from a burning hive.

Finally out of the tear gas, Cally staggered across the stone terrace toward the wide, curving stairs that led to the gardens below.

"Fire!"

Cally looked up just in time to see dozens of crossbow arrows flying toward the terrace. She ducked, putting a marble replica of the *Venus de Milo* between her and the deadly rain. As she watched from her hiding place, she saw one of the other guests jump atop the balustrade's railing, instantly shapeshifting into his winged form.

With a beat of his eight-foot wings, the transformed vampire shot up into the night sky in a desperate attempt to escape the Van Helsings' crossbows before they could reload. It looked like he had succeeded, but then a shadow soared from the roofline of the building.

With just a few beats of its own leathery wings, the gargoyle easily overtook the fleeing vampire, who screamed as the beast's slashing talons destroyed his right wing. Unable to maintain balance, the vampire spun out of control and crashed a hundred feet down into the hedges that ringed the gardens.

Cally's guts tightened as she listened to the gargoyle shriek in triumph. Things had just gotten a whole lot worse: both the Van Helsings and their pet gargoyle were out for blood.

* * *

Lilith pushed her way out onto the terrace, literally climbing over her fellow guests to escape the smoke-filled confines of the ballroom. With her gown in tatters and black tears streaking her face, she no longer looked like the vampire debutante who had held every eye in the room.

"Jules! Mom! Daddy! Where are you?" she cried out, hoping to spot a familiar face in the surrounding crowd.

"Lilith! Look out!"

Lilith turned to find the last person in the world she wanted to see, Cally Monture, cowering behind a statue, pointing at something in the sky. She heard the sound of wings—*big wings*—coming up from behind her. Lilith spun around to see something that looked like a cross between a pit bull and a crocodile bearing down on her, talons outstretched. She screamed as the gargoyle snatched her up in its claws and bore her into the night sky.

"Let go!" Lilith shrieked, struggling to free herself from the gargoyle's viselike grip. "Help! Help me!"

In response to her cry, something large and gray landed on the gargoyle's back and yanked on the loop of heavy chain encircling the beast's throat, turning the collar into a makeshift garrote.

Lilith thought she was being rescued by her father or Jules in winged form, but when she got a good look at the hideous creature riding the gargoyle's back, she wasn't sure if it had come to rescue her or was simply fighting for its share of the spoils.

The gargoyle snarled as it tried to unseat its unwanted passenger, but the mystery flier proved unshakable, hanging on to the chain around the beast's neck like a rodeo rider atop a raging bull. Roaring in pain and anger, the gargoyle let go of Lilith, sending her plummeting to the earth fifty feet below.

As the ground zoomed up to meet her, Lilith realized she had neither the time nor the skill to shapeshift into her winged form quickly enough to avoid being hurt. Even though a fall from such a height wouldn't kill a vampire, it would hurt a *whole lot*. And if she smashed her skull hard enough to damage her brain, the injuries could very well prove permanent, even with her near-instantaneous regenerative ability. All she could do was close her eyes and scream.

Just as she was about to smash into the marble paving stones of the terrace, a figure darted forward and caught her in its outstretched arms. Lilith spread the fingers covering her face to peep out at her savior, expecting to see Jules's handsome face. Instead, she was greeted by someone totally unexpected.

"Exo?" Lilith gasped in amazement.

Xander Orlock, son of Count Boris Orlock, flashed a relieved smile as he put her back on her feet. He turned and shouted to his cousin, who was hurrying in their direction.

"Make sure Lilith gets to safety!"

"Sure thing, cuz!" Jules said, taking Lilith by the arm.

"What about you?" Lilith asked, looking over her shoulder at Xander.

He pointed to where the gargoyle and the mystery flier fought in midair like a pair of sparring hawks. "I'm going to help Klaus take care of business." With that, Xander transformed into his winged form and, with a single beat of his wings, flew up to join the battle raging overhead.

"Come on, Lili—you heard Exo," Jules said, dragging her back to the relative safety of the ballroom. "We've got to get out of here!"

"Who's Klaus?" Lilith asked as she watched Xander's hell-bat form strike the gargoyle from the other direction.

"That is." Jules pointed to the creature battling the gargoyle. "He's Xander's older brother."

Can't get enough of Cally and Lilith?

Watch for the next
Vamps novel.